DEATH IN CLOSE-UP

Also by Nancy Livingston:

DEATH IN CLOSE-UP

by

Nancy Livingston

St. Martin's Press
New York

This book is dedicated to my PA *colleagues every-where, unsung heroines, almost everyone.*

Library of Congress Cataloging-in-Publication Data

Livingston, Nancy.
      Death in close-up / Nancy Livingston.
          p.   cm.
     ISBN 0-312-04296-5
     I. Title.
   PR6062.I915D38   1990
   823'.914—dc20   89-77922
                                           CIP

First published in Great Britain by Victor Gollancz Ltd.

First U.S. Edition
10 9 8 7 6 5 4 3 2 1

PROLOGUE

It was an anonymous house in Blake Road, Hendon, a semi-detached built between the wars with nothing to recommend it. When first built, a pair of newly weds had served it slavishly. They'd spent every penny colour-washing the walls duck-egg blue, buying tub chairs and chintz to match. The families that followed weren't so houseproud. During their occupation, as roads began to bisect north London, increasing dirt and noise meant they lost interest.

Life continued. Number 5A changed hands every decade or so until one particular family moved in: a man, his wife and their small daughter. Twenty-four years later those three human beings had been reduced to one.

The man lay fully dressed on the shabby candlewick bedspread, as was his habit, and stared at the ceiling. He no longer noticed the busy arterial traffic. For him the house was silent, full of memories, without warmth or life since his daughter Anne had been killed.

He'd lived on here after his wife had walked out on them, bringing up the child alone. Despite initial unhappiness, he discovered he didn't really care about Margery. What mattered was Anne. When he returned from work she would always be there, peeping through the bars of the gate on the lookout for him.

He'd found a homely neighbour to act as a child-minder, and she'd helped him nurse Anne through measles and chickenpox. He'd watched his skinny daughter grow; never pretty, there was too much of him in her for that, but in her shy, self-contained way, a delight.

After secretarial college, she'd got herself an excellent job. They'd been planning to celebrate that the night her life had been cut short, nearly five years ago. Over one thousand, seven hundred and thirty days. It was ironic the way the judge referred to it as a tragic accident. The man knew differently. Accidents could happen, but not like that. Anne's photograph was on the bedside table. Another hung on the wall, but her father didn't need either to recall her dead face, how she'd looked in the mortuary.

He'd fought against hatred. He tried to forgive, but he'd stopped attending church weeks ago when the realization of what he must do had come as a revelation. It had washed away tension, leaving him a weak and empty vessel. His strength would return once the task was finished; he believed that passionately. Only then would he know real peace. And God had shown him the way. There was relief now the time had come to act. Strangers might call it retribution; an eye for an eye, a life for a life — for him it was simply justice.

1

INCISION IN THE THORAX

Rainbow Television. Monday morning
Of the three people facing the bank of screens in Studio A
control room, only one was excited, but he more than made up
for the other two. Adrenalin forced its way through his stiffening
arteries, surprising tired blood vessels, and he wriggled with such
ecstasy at being creative, the seat of his trousers took on a new
sheen.

"Go in, four! Go in, go in, go in — HOLD IT."

On screen, the lethargic zoom-in on camera four ended
abruptly in a badly framed close-up of a once-famous face.

The director was incandescent by this time. Sweat poured
from him as the effort of making his small talent stretch too far
took its toll. Beside him, the vision mixer read a magazine to
combat boredom but the PA, Pat, was attentive. She clicked off
her stop-watch having decided, correctly, that the shot had gone
on long enough.

"Tape run. Stand by to cue Jacinta. Eighty-eight on three next.
Ready with the roller, standby grams."

There was more than resignation in her voice, there was the
absolute certainty that this prat would never finish.

"Hang on! I haven't said whether *I'm* satisfied." Excitement
was replaced by irritation. "Robert, is Make-up about?"

A disembodied voice answered through the loudspeaker panel.

"Standing beside me, Bernard. Is it the blood?"

"It certainly is. According to the script, Margarite should have
a *bruise* and a slight *trickle* down one cheek, not be awash with
the stuff. Second point, Margarite forgot to open her eyes and do
her little moan. Did she get a cue?"

"Affirmative," replied the floor manager. "I prodded her foot
as the camera tracked past."

"Well, remind her again. Get that mess cleaned up and reset from the top." Bernard rounded on his PA. "I don't care if we are running out of time, no one rolls the roller until I give the —"

"Christ!"

"Robert? What's the matter?" The scream had frozen all activity. They stared at the screens. The floor manager had pulled the bedcover back and revealed the source of the blood. The actress, Margarite Pelouse, sported a realistic-looking chest wound with the weapon still in place. The director was outraged.

"What does she think she's playing at? This is no time for a joke! Her character's been knocked down by a car, not —"

"I think she's dead." Robert was high-pitched with fear, but they were immune to reality in the control room.

"Not until the end of the scene! That's when she opens her eyes, gives the little moan as rehearsed, and dies."

"No, *dead*, Bernard! Dead dead."

"Dead dead?"

"Yes!"

"Good Lord!" There was a moment of complete stupefaction, then the PA saw the clock. They were within seconds of an over-run which would take everyone (well, almost everyone) into overtime.

"Lunch!" she croaked automatically. "Clear the studio."

The police car blared to a halt in answer to the 999 call. The driver reported the situation and called for reinforcements in a few terse sentences. He was already too late. Cast and crew of *Doctors and Nurses* at Rainbow Television's Soho studios, most of them still unaware of what had happened, had melted into the crowds in Oxford Street.

Programme controller's office
The office had creamy leather furniture and carpets, bowls of lavender, plus an imitation fireplace in pale York stone with blazing gas-fired coals. It was designed as a soothing backdrop to creativity, not the belligerent interview that was now taking place.

Anger surged through DS Mullin's fingertips, giving his hands a life of their own. They begged so hard to be allowed to strangle someone, he was forced to hide their indiscretion in his pockets.

"Why on earth was everyone allowed to leave before we got here?" He was too large for the chair, on secondment to the team whose footsteps now echoed through the near-empty studios, an outsider of whom the rest were suspicious. His task was simply to obtain names and addresses of the few who'd remained on the premises, but DS Mullin intended to do more than that. A suspicious death was his chance to make his mark and witnesses must be made to divulge every scrap of information.

Ashley Fallowfield, one time chorus-boy, TV announcer, personality and now programme controller at Rainbow Television replied wearily, "Utter the word 'lunch' and lemmings could get flattened in the rush."

"But by then you knew the actress had been killed!"

"It's a hospital series, it happens every episode —"

"We're not talking about television, Mr Fallowfield."

"Look . . ." Ashley's migraine was giving him hell. "When they heard the PA shout, they went like Pavlov's dogs because they always do, but they'll be back soon. It's nearly half past two and we start again on cameras at three."

"Including the murderer?" Mullin was from Leicester and didn't enjoy talking to men who wore mascara.

"Whoever did it won't want to lose half a day's pay," Ashley said innocently.

"Mr Fallowfield, you don't seem to understand . . . reality has taken over from fiction. We are investigating a suspicious death — a woman has been stabbed!" The programme controller pursed his lips.

"Margarite would prefer being referred to as a lady."

"Mr Fallowfield!"

"Petal, I cannot pretend what I do not feel. I know someone's been naughty but he'll get a vote of thanks from the profession. Margarite Pelouse was not well liked."

"It is customary not to speak ill of the dead," Mullin said with distaste.

"You won't find many shedding tears," Ashley Fallowfield was

9

sincere. "But give credit where it's due, her death's an absolute Godsend as far as the ratings are concerned. Once this gets out we'll beat *EastEnders*, you see if we don't. The network is bound to want another series after that." The representative of law'n order stared.

"You weren't thinking of transmitting the scene?"

"Every last frame, petal," Ashley lifted up pious eyes, "as a tribute to a great lady of the theatre. The editor is reworking the rest of the script to make it fit."

The sergeant wondered what his superior's view would be about that. "May I ask you how long these studios have been in existence?"

"Six months thanks to Hilda of England. She wanted competition and companies like this sprang up like toadstools. They depend on people like myself, though. I'm one of a dying breed, Sergeant, someone who actually knows how to make television programmes." Ashley left a pause sufficient for Mullin to marvel. "Did you ever raid this place when it was a cinema? They used to show porn movies. No? Anyway, it was bought by a consortium who converted it and one of them bumped into me at BAFTA, asked what you actually *did* once you owned a studio — it was when Central were recording the last episode of *Crossroads* — and I gave them a priceless piece of advice: 'Buy those motel sets,' I said, 'and you'll never look back.'"

Despite himself, Mullin asked, "How come?"

"Scenery is the most expensive item in any programme budget, take my word for it. So there they were, having founded Rainbow Television and with masses of little sets with beds in them, which solved the problem of what to do next."

"A hospital series?" Ashley nodded approvingly.

"Based on the NHS?" Ashley shuddered.

"Thanks to Hilda, your NHS is a dead duck fit only for documentaries. *Doctors and Nurses* is about *private* medicine and the viewers love it. Hilda should be pleased; it encourages their aspirations. It's transmitted three times a week at six thirty p.m. on Channel 4."

"What part did Margarite Pelouse play?"

"She was this week's guest star. The Monday episode always features an 'unknown patient'. By Wednesday we reveal who it is. We've used half the old has-beens in the business — they're cheap and our viewers are old enough to remember when they were famous. In this story one of the nurses is looking for the mother who handed her over for adoption years ago, and this woman is brought into Casualty, suffering from amnesia —"

"Just a minute . . ." The big sergeant refused to be swept along, "Private hospitals don't have Casualty departments."

"Oh, do me a favour!" Ashley said indignantly. "What else could we have done with the motel reception set? Anyway, you've got to have Casualty scenes in a hospital series, the public expect it."

"When did Miss Pelouse begin rehearsing?"

"Only three days ago, actually. It's all rather odd — another actress was due to play the part but she broke her hip, poor love. That's the snag when you use old faithfuls, some of them are rather fragile. Not Margarite, of course. To be honest, I'd have preferred not to have her as a replacement. I guessed it would mean trouble, but it was short notice."

"Why use her if she was such a nuisance?" Ashley looked at him pityingly.

"Because she was a genius, petal. On stage, television, wherever — *audiences* adored her. And of course there was always the chance of publicity because of . . ." Ashley changed his mind and continued quickly, "Generally speaking, geniuses aren't nice people, they're a pain in the proverbial, but in our business you learn to put up with that."

"And have you any idea why she was killed?" Ashley's eyes were at their widest.

"My God, what a question! Everyone who ever met her ended up wanting to do that."

Studio A. Prop store
Round every studio, store rooms cluster; dingy, chilly, full of junk, just brick walls illuminated by bare bulbs. Studio A Prop store had the familiar crowded look of a second-hand shop. At one end, Detective Inspector Newton had established a tem-

porary interview room. It was far enough away from the studio and for added privacy, the property master had provided a couple of Victorian screens.

He approved the shabby no-nonsense atmosphere, but had he had the choice, Frank Newton would have chosen a different desk. The prop master had obliged with one from the consultant's office set and Newton sat behind it uncomfortably, waiting for Robert, the floor manager, to recover. He wondered if real Harley Street consultants went in for such luxury? His elderly GP managed with a Formica-topped table.

As a CID Inspector in a turbulent area of London, he'd long ago trained himself to appear impassive. Last week a drug abuser had fallen (been pushed?) under a train at Oxford Circus station. When he'd viewed the remains, as usual DI Newton felt sick, but no one there had guessed. Today, as senior investigating officer called to a suspicious death in a TV studio, he'd discovered the worst possible situation; a large floor containing approximately a dozen exit points through which a constant stream of people had access. The sets were closely packed, isolating people from one another. Witnesses would be a premium. The final blow had been to discover everyone had been permitted to leave the studio before he had arrived. Newton had almost let his temper rip when he'd heard that.

Instead, the police machine had been set in motion very rapidly indeed. It hadn't taken more than minutes to obtain authorization for an incident room to be set up. Meanwhile, Scene-of-Crime was already videoing the remains. Newton requested an Exhibits officer to cope with the hundreds of property items scattered over the sets, and in addition to the outsider Mullin, DPWs Mackenzie and Dexter were collecting personal details from those now drifting back from lunch. Most of the crew and cast appeared genuinely unaware of the killing. Those who'd seen the shot on screen had, like the director, assumed it was some kind of practical joke. Those who had grasped the reality, however, had obviously been discussing it avidly and for that reason it couldn't be kept secret much longer.

Newton wanted to make the most of the small breathing space nevertheless. He waited patiently for the floor manager to begin.

12

At least he'd had the common sense to remain on the premises, but it was taking a while for him to come to terms with the violence.

The scene was still vivid in Robert's mind: Margarite's silver-gilt hair fanned over the pillow and the bloody chest wound with the handle of a knife protruding from it. He was amazed at the calm, passive figure behind the desk. Quiet and aloof, hands clasped, DI Newton regarded him as though there was all the time in the world.

The floor manager made an effort. "Sorry I can't stop twitching . . . I realized it wasn't a joke when I could *smell* the blood. The stuff we use isn't the same at all."

"Try and put that out of your mind," Newton advised. "Concentrate on the order of events. Where was Miss Pelouse immediately before she took up her position on the bed?"

"Margarite used the quick-change dressing room to rest in. Elderly artistes prefer it. It's a tent," Robert pointed to the square marked on the studio plan, "tucked in the corner next to Wardrobe. Margarite waited in there until she was needed. She'd been allocated the pukka number one dressing room of course, but that's a whole flight of stairs away from the studio."

"Was she alone in the tent?"

The fair head shook, "Neglect Margarite and she'd throw a wobbly."

"Who was with her?"

If I were casting *The Bill*, thought the floor manager, I'd never pick this one; mournful looking eyes, sallow complexion, dandruff . . . !

"Apart from the make-up girl and her dresser, there was Jason." Eyebrows lifted fractionally. "Jason Cornish." He saw Newton pick up the cast list. "You won't find him on that, he's a model. He was Margarite's latest toy . . . her friend."

"Where is he now?"

"Sobbing his heart out to the *Sun* when I last saw him."

Without being bidden, the detective constable who'd been taking notes, got up quickly. Newton's instruction was curt.

"Find Mullin, tell him to put the fear of God into him."

"Sir." The constable disappeared. Robert shrugged.

"Justin's the last person you should worry about. He's an ageing model and Margarite was his meal ticket."

"It's necessary to follow procedure, sir. Until Miss Pelouse's relatives have been informed, no one on this site is permitted to speak to the media." Robert opened his mouth then changed his mind. If the police believed the secret would be kept they must be fools, but he wouldn't be the one to point that out.

"What happened from the time Miss Pelouse left the changing tent?" asked Newton.

"The call-boy took her to the Intensive Care Unit set. Make-up did the usual titivating, the stage-manager wired Margarite up to the machinery — all pretend, you understand? Then the call-boy pulled the screens into position and they left her. I was cueing the previous scene in the corridor set when the call-boy reported she was ready."

"And alone?"

"Yes. When camera four tracked round the edge of the screen Margarite was as we expected to see her, apart from blood on the sheets. We hadn't bothered to rehearse. We'd gone straight for a take because we were within minutes of the lunchbreak. I called 'action', that's all the warning an old pro needs."

"Where's the set on this plan?"

"It's this area here, marked ICU. Just two walls at right angles; one has the bed with all the medical gubbins attached and the other has a door which opens on to a false corridor — a painted backcloth hung on the studio wall. We use screens to conceal the lack of a third or fourth wall."

"This door, was it locked?" Robert shook his head.

"It has to be practical, it's used by everyone entering the set. After Margarite had done her little sigh we were supposed to do a tape run during which we repositioned camera four and pulled a screen further round. Then we should've picked up with a low shot over Margarite's body, of the door. That's when Jacinta Charles, she's one of the nurses and in this episode she's discovered she's Margarite's illegitimate daughter, should have dashed in, grabbed her hand and said, 'It's me, Mother, please don't leave me now'. Cut to a two-shot on camera two who'd poked his lens through the door — which had been deliberately left ajar — cue Jacinta to bow her head and weep, mix back to four to do a tilt down of Margarite's face against the pillow, freeze frame and super end captions. It wasn't what you'd call original, Inspector. More tried and true." Newton sorted out the essentials.

"Was Miss Charles in her position behind the door?" Robert hesitated.

"It's tales out of school," he mumbled.

"Not when there's been a murder, sir."

"Jacinta's a lovely girl, but she's having a bit of a ding-dong with one of the cameramen. We have to prise them apart when it's time for her entrance."

"I repeat my question: was Miss Charles behind the door when you called out that Miss Pelouse was dead?"

"I don't think so." After his initial hesitancy, Robert became garrulous. "I'd forgotten to tell the call-boy to warn her, to be honest. I remember crossing my fingers when we began, hoping by some miracle she'd be in position. After I'd yelled Margarite was dead, various people came rushing on to the set to find out what the fuss was about, but not Jacinta. Presumably she was still with Simon." It sounded plausible, but for some reason Newton felt it didn't ring true.

"You can give me the names of the others in a moment. So, while you were busy elsewhere anyone could have entered this set and be hidden by the screens?"

"I suppose so. They certainly shielded the bed from the rest of the studio. But what I can't understand — why didn't Margarite cry out? I mean, with so many of us about?" Newton was also extremely curious about that.

"How long was Miss Pelouse left alone?"

"I wanted to allow enough time to settle her in position, but she was there longer than I'd intended. Part of the wall fell down in the corridor set and we had to do shots eighty-five and eighty-six twice."

"How much time do you usually allow?"

"Margarite didn't like to be rushed but five minutes would have been ample. She must have been there over quarter of an hour in the end. We'd got the scenery back in position very

15

quickly but it took several minutes for Bernard to calm down. He panics nowadays — it's probably his age." Inside this young man was a television director struggling for recognition, Newton decided.

"What caused the scenery to fall?"

"That was pure accident. A porter, one of the extras, had to rush a stretcher down the corridor, interrupting a love scene. He bumped into a wall before he could stop himself."

"A noisy scene then?" Newton said thoughtfully.

"Very. We shove everyone who's available through the corridor scenes. Good production value."

"And — brief?"

"This week, yes. Those love scenes are our buffer. If we're all right for time — each episode has to run twenty-four minutes thirty seconds by the way — Nurse Simmons and Dr Nettleton just meet, say 'Hi', and that's it. If we're under-running, they yatter away for as long as we need before going into a clinch —"

"In a corridor?" Newton asked incredulously.

"Usually it's the sluice room. Their storyline will continue until one of them asks for more money then they'll be written out," Robert predicted confidently. "That's how it works in a soap."

"And that particular scene this week, had it gone smoothly, would have taken how long?"

"Approximately three minutes plus another minute to settle the studio and roll the recording tape. The PA can give you an accurate estimate." It was near enough for Newton: the killer had either planned to be extremely quick or had been fortunate.

"How many people were there altogether?" The floor manager checked them off.

"Eight in the cast, ten extras — I sent them for an early lunch as soon as we'd finished in the corridor. It helps keep the noise level down."

"What about the crew?"

"Thirty to thirty-five; it varies." The mournful eyes suddenly looked up at him.

"Had Miss Pelouse any enemies?" Robert laughed before he could stop himself.

"Just about everyone who ever worked with her."

Great, thought Detective Inspector Newton.

Rainbow Television. Star dressing room

There had been an attempt at glamour but the effort hadn't been sustained. The first incumbent, a fading Hollywood star, declared yellow was the only colour which gave her inspiration, but buttercup paint had long since flaked off the hastily plastered walls which hadn't been allowed time to dry. Striped curtains and shaggy yellow carpet were speckled with London dust and now the dressing room had a tawdry atmosphere. Jason Cornish noticed neither dust nor décor. He was intent on making a certain discovery before the police beat him to it. He didn't hear them enter, but when he looked up, two solid figures were reflected in the brightly lit mirror. As one of them shut the door he tried to hide his discomfiture.

Half an hour previously, Jason had ducked out of sight and hidden in Margarite's dressing room. Equally instinctively, he'd resorted to the brandy she kept in her dressing case. Then, as survival reasserted itself, he'd engaged in a fruitful conversation with a journalist, regaining enough composure to haggle over the price of the scoop.

Self-preservation had guided Jason all his life. He'd eased himself unscarred through Bermondsey school playgrounds because he'd learned early that handsome features were a good little earner. His formative years were spent advertising gooey synthetic foods, spitting out each repellent mouthful as soon as camera shutter clicked because spots would have been a disaster.

As his income had increased via knitting patterns to international menswear, so had Jason's appetite for the better things in life. He neglected diet and attention to face and figure until the day when nemesis overtook him: a message from his agent confirmed that neither the French nor Italians required his services that season. Jason Cornish's modelling career was at an end.

He'd been drowning his sorrows when Margarite walked into his life. He'd let her make the running at first, but when he excused himself and went to the Gents, he'd changed his mind.

17

Cruel strip lights emphasized the thinning hair, the crêpey wrinkled skin and extra poundage round his once-slim hips. His bank account was empty, he hadn't the rent. The time had come to take out life assurance. Jason braced himself and returned to the bar.

It had been far worse than he could have imagined. He'd needed a diplomat's skill at times to calm friends and strangers alike after Margarite's worst efforts. In return, once she was penitent, his own demands had increased. In six months he'd built up a nice little nest egg and if it was now over — so what? There were other wealthy old divorcees. The money would see him through for a couple of months, even provide a holiday. As long as he was seen in the right places, Jason Cornish would find himself another meal ticket, and this time he wouldn't rush. He'd find out if the bitch had a mean streak first.

Calm again, with his wits sharp enough to look after number one, Jason began to search Margarite's ancient Vuitton suitcase and handbag because there was a very useful cheque hidden somewhere, one he'd swear she hadn't had the time to hand to the intended recipient. Now two CID men stood foursquare staring at him with cold suspicion.

"Sorry to intrude, Mr Cornish . . ." Mullin was acid. "I understand you've been talking to the Press?" The threat the voice conveyed revived a memory of a boy who'd once thrust a broken bottle dangerously near his face. The second man moved so swiftly, it took Jason by surprise.

"This your suitcase?" The gold initials MEP glittered spitefully. The constable reached out a hand. "We'll look after that too, sir." Wordlessly, Jason handed over the wallet. He knew it contained over a hundred pounds in cash, possibly the missing cheque as well. He considered demanding it back when DS Mullin's next question banished all such temptation.

"How was it you knew Miss Pelouse had been killed before anyone else did, Mr Cornish?"

"I didn't! I — I overheard one of the cameramen talking about it, that's all."

"Really, sir? I hope you can identify him for us. As far as we are aware, only the man on camera four knew and he remained with the floor manager." This was baldly true because the crew hadn't yet been interviewed, but in his panic Jason Cornish didn't stop to reason matters out.

"You can't think that I had anything to do with . . . ?" Mullin gave a slow, hard smile.

"Well now, Mr Cornish . . . look at it from our point of view. You were an intimate friend of the deceased. You knew exactly when she'd be on her own, and when she's discovered brutally stabbed to death, what do you do, sir? Are you so distressed you're too shocked to speak? No, you're not. You're on the blower to the newspapers and when we walk in you're holding a wallet which doesn't belong to you. Now what I want you to do is give the constable here an exact account of your movements and if we find your prints on the murder weapon —"

"They couldn't possibly be! I never touched it! Why should I want to kill Margarite?"

"If you wanted to get rid of her you might, Mr Cornish. It's the usual reason for a murder. So you tell the constable your version and don't think of making any more calls, sir. In your position, it wouldn't be wise."

And Mullin departed, having conscientiously carried out Newton's instructions.

Rainbow Television. Master Control

It was the hub of the studio operation where the recording machinery was housed. In one of the small, air-conditioned cubicles, far too many people huddled round a black and white monitor. Crouched in front of it, his face almost up against the glass, an engineer adjusted the controls.

Those watchers who spilled out into the maintenance area, shuffled or stood on tiptoe, mesmerized by the fuzzy, ill-lit picture. Someone demanded, "Can't you make it sharper?" and the engineer tweaked obediently. Immediately, the scene on the studio floor came into black and white focus. Another one whispered, "I think I'm going to be sick!" but nobody moved.

"I say . . . do they always do that when you die?"

"Only if you get bumped off. Just make sure it doesn't happen to you."

19

"Easier said than done these days. Here, what's he going to do with that?"

"You can tell how long she's been dead by taking the temperature."

"Yes but why use such a huge thing . . . Ooh, he's not going to shove it up there!"

"We know how long. She was killed before the meal break."

"Yes, but *they* don't know, they weren't here. Aw, what a liberty! Margarite would've had *him* by the balls if she'd been alive."

"She'll come back and haunt him, you'll see."

DPW Dexter crashed into the temporary interview room without even knocking. DI Newton started up angrily.

"Sorry, sir. I thought you ought to know immediately. They're watching what's going on."

"Who are? Where?" A dreadful suspicion was about to be confirmed.

"The technical people. There's a remote camera suspended from the gantry as part of the security system. It enables engineers to scan the studio floor —" But DI Newton had already gone, like a bolt from a crossbow.

Programme controller's office
Ashley Fallowfield was disgruntled. He couldn't understand why no one was being nice to him any more. He'd done his best to co-operate, bent over backwards (metaphorically speaking: these were *real* policemen after all). He'd answered one damn boring question after another until he wanted to scream at the big butch one. Now there were three more stamping all over his lovely cream carpet, shouting their heads off like there'd been a crime or something.

They'd got their knickers in a twist over the crew. The most important one, whose dreadful suit made Ashley feel sad and who looked remarkably like a spaniel, had turned very nasty indeed. If he didn't stop barking soon, Ashley's nerves would be in crisis.

"I refuse to be held responsible for everything that happens on these premises," he said sulkily. "What d'you expect in a TV studio — privacy?"

"I don't expect to find employees snooping on a police investigation! I demand a modicum of decency and integrity."

Oh come on, petal! thought Ashley, who's a silly old copper? Aloud he said, "There's none of that here. Or at Scotland Yard if half what you read in the papers is true."

"I ordered that studio to be cleared!" DI Newton sounded dangerous.

"It was cleared," Ashley soothed, frightened by his anger. "That's why they all pushed off to Master Control. You'd forbidden them to leave the building, the bar was closed, what else d'you expect the crew to do?"

"I'd also forbidden them to interfere!"

"They weren't interfering! They were interested, that's all. As a matter of fact, I was watching myself," he said placidly. He indicated the large set in the corner of the room, "All the studio outputs can be patched through to this office, it helps me keep a necessary eye. I must say one or two of your lot are very good. Far better than *Crime Watch*."

"Have Miss Pelouse's next of kin been informed?" asked Newton heavily.

"Some of them."

"Pardon?"

"Margarite had had three husbands apart from her boyfriends. She might have been old but that didn't stop her. Nympho. One of her little foibles . . . As to which of them was her nearest and dearest at this moment in time, who can say?"

"Is her current husband still living?"

"Willie was her last and they divorced quite a while ago. *He's* married to Melissa thing these days, at least I think he is. When he rang, I forgot to ask." The detective inspector stared, uncomprehendingly.

"Willie heard about it on the news," Ashley explained.

"You mean . . . ?"

"Now listen, petal, VTR were already recording the scene, remember. When Robert yelled Margarite was dead, those

21

engineers moved like lightning. They fed the sequence down the line to every company in the network. Not the BBC, of course, that's against the rules. ITN put out a thirty second newsflash and there's nothing you can do once that's happened."

"I forbade anyone to release the information!"

"How was I to know the engineers would work their meal break? They never have before. They've done you a VHS copy by the way, which you can keep. Worth five quid, a cassette is," Ashley offered generously.

"You'll be given a receipt, Mr Fallowfield. The item will be returned to these premises, in due course."

"Suit yourself," he shrugged, then asked, "how much longer? We need to begin recording again, you know. Bernard's ever so worried. We've another fifty pages to do before the wrap — and I've had the conceptual director on the phone."

"Who?"

"The money man. Called himself an 'investment analyst' before, but had to nip out of the city ahead of the Fraud Squad. Gave himself that poncy title when he switched to television. They're like that in the consortium, crooked. Don't even trust each other half the time but they all rely on me to keep *Doctors and Nurses* on schedule, so how much longer?"

Newton stared at the pink, plump face with its frame of gilded curls and made another attempt to get his message across.

"I must emphasize again, Mr Fallowfield, we are conducting a murder investigation. A painstaking business that cannot be rushed."

"Why not let us help?" Ashley was luminous with enthusiasm. "Two of our cast were in the *Miss Marple* series —one even played a policeman — he'd know what to do."

Newton realized he must either leave or break the rule of a lifetime and lose his temper. Ashley was hurt. His final puzzled attempt at friendliness floated after them down the passage.

"I've always wanted to become a mason — is it difficult to join?"

Studio A. Prop store/interview room
Behind the Victorian screens, the police had gathered in gloomy

22

resignation. Newton addressed them, conscious of keeping himself under tight control.

"They're not defective, they're people who work in television. Grown-up children is the best way to think of them." Round the desk there were nods of agreement from the rest of the team.

"It was as if it was part of this week's episode," DPW Dexter shook her head despairingly. "Most of them will keep insisting the victim deserved to die."

"No one ever deserved to die. Let's get started. First information is that the deceased was alone for about fifteen minutes with a noisy scene going on in the corridor set — shown here on the plan — separated from the ICU set by . . . Nurse Williams's room and Dr Watkins's bedsit . . .

"Doc Pavis's initial assessment is that the killer probably clamped one hand over the victim's mouth and stabbed with the other. She presumably recognized whoever it was which is why she didn't cry out. How far have you got?" Newton directed his question at DPW Mackenzie who had the best legs in the division; it comforted him to look at them.

"I've told those who've returned to stay in their dressing rooms for the present. The ones involved in the corridor set claim they didn't know what had happened. When they were told they could go to lunch, they thought what they'd seen on screen was some sort of joke. I think they're telling the truth, even if they are actors. The crew who had headsets on were aware of course."

"Which didn't stop them leaving the site as well," Newton grumbled. "Keep everyone here from now on until I give permission to leave."

"Yes, sir."

"The snag is, Guv," Mullin understood this familiarity was encouraged in the Met, "in this place, actors wander in and out of make-up and wardrobe rooms and these open directly on to the studio floor."

"Thank you, Sergeant." Mullin mistakenly took this for encouragement.

"It's the same with the crew. *They* go in and out with technical equipment or push off to make the odd phone call during breaks in the recording."

"No doubt it's going to mean extra work cross-checking statements," said DI Newton sharply, "but I don't care if it was like Oxford Circus in the rush hour, I intend to find out where everyone was during the vital period, right?"

"Could I ask a question?" It was Mullin again. "What exactly is an 'extra'?"

"Rent-a-crowd," Newton replied briefly. "If they talk close to camera no sound comes out because they don't have any lines."

"And they're ordered by size," Sylvia Mackenzie had inside information. "A ward sister always has to be size fourteen because of the uniform." Newton's eyebrows went up.

"Sure they're not having you on, Sylvia?"

"No, sir. The production assistant was adamant. Costumes are stock items and extras are ordered from agencies, to fit. Whenever a non-speaking ward sister is seen in *Doctors and Nurses*, she is always a size fourteen. And black."

"Black?"

"Ethnic balance, to please the IBA."

"Nothing would surprise me any more," Newton sighed. "Has anyone so far, of whatever persuasion, come up with anything useful? Like why the victim was killed?" The group shook their heads again.

"By all accounts, she wasn't well liked," the young detective constable volunteered.

"There are degrees of dislike. Today someone felt the urge to stab Margarite Pelouse full of holes, that's quite different. Did any cast or crew claim to have seen anyone else in the vicinity of the ICU set? Some of you must've picked up a few crumbs?" DPW Doreen Dexter, solidly built with no beguiling attributes to distract him, referred to her notebook.

"I asked the stage-manager, Alix Baxter, to make a visual check of her props in my presence. They're kept in a metal cage for which she has the key, but it's left unlocked during the recording period. As far as she could ascertain, three items were missing: a photograph in a silver-coloured frame, a box of tissues, both of which Miss Baxter claimed were normal pilferage, and one from a set of surgical instruments, a breast knife. I informed both Dr Pavis and the Exhibits officer as soon as he arrived."

DI Newton thumped the desk, letting slip his sang-froid. "They've no business giving actors things like that to play with! Right, let's get back to it. I want a complete list of names and addresses before we leave, plus precise details of where everyone was when . . ." He paused in dialling a number. "Why isn't this thing working?"

"It's a prop, sir. The real one's over there, screwed to the wall."

Newton shoved the offending phone aside. "Bloody Alice in Wonderland!"

2

ENTER A GERIATRIC

Oxford Circus tube station. Monday afternoon
A nondescript, slightly stooped man wearing a mac and carrying
an attaché case and brolly, was swept forward with the crowd up
the steps into Regent Street, north. He turned left, crossed Great
Castle Street, past British Home Stores, and rounded the corner
into Cavendish Square. He'd reached an age when the small
pleasures in life made the day a little brighter and thoughts of
what was to come quickened his pace.

The invention of the microchip never ceased to impress G D H
Pringle. Born of a generation who understood the abacus,
educated to use a slide rule and finally, thankful to have an
adding machine at his disposal, he had retired from the Inland
Revenue before it received an allocation of the latest of
mankind's miracles. He'd left with few regrets however, obeying
the stern exhortation of the decade to make way for a younger
man.

There followed a few idyllic years when he'd half convinced
himself he was a gentleman of leisure and independent means.
Time had eroded both illusions. Mr Pringle might dream that he
was still in early middle-age, but a form had arrived, sere and
yellow, reminding him he was sixty-five. Senior citizenship: the
door which stands ajar but has no handle on the other side.

Mr Pringle was not disturbed by the new status so much as his
immediate circumstances. He'd once believed the additional
widower's pension to which he was now entitled would com-
pensate for inflation. He'd been disillusioned. His Revenue
pension was index-linked, but it was amazing how far the gap had
widened between expectation and reality. Since retiring he'd
been rash in the art market and depleted his savings. None of this
would have mattered, he could have managed, had it not been

26

for the roof. This was in such a parlous state that unless he earned extra money quickly, he might end up in a pickle.

He'd ignored the leak for years. A bucket strategically placed had been sufficient, but last month his Help threatened to leave. The bucket had overflowed once too often and his carpets now had an offensive odour, she declared. Mr Pringle consulted newspaper advertisements and summoned two professional gentlemen to give quotes.

After their visit there followed a night of doubt and sorrow. Doubt that he could afford a watertight roof and sorrow that he'd been so profligate as to indulge in a hobby. In the dawn, over a cup of tea, Mr Pringle considered parting with one of his pictures. Strength returned with his boiled egg. He was damned if he'd spoil his small collection. Now was the time to use his former skills. He would advertise his services to members of the human race unable to complete their tax returns.

His friend, Mrs Bignell, pinned the first of his postcards above her bar in The Bricklayers. For a fortnight he was inundated, and a corner of the saloon became his office, but when the rush was over he discovered he'd scarcely earned enough for new tiles! The words of one of the roofing contractors were engraved in his memory: "Once we strip the old ones off, squire, gawd knows what mischief we'll discover underneath . . ." Mr Pringle knew he must exert himself.

He circulated postcards to all those in his address book. His hand had wavered over "Fallowfield", but he reminded himself beggars couldn't be choosy — and Ashley had contacted him by return.

There were certain aspects of Fallowfield's character which Mr Pringle recalled as he travelled into London on the tube. He pushed them aside. There was another more urgent matter to be dealt with first. One of The Bricklayers's clients had paid by cheque and Mavis Bignell's look of reproach when he had told her brought a chill to Mr Pringle's veins. "A cheque? Lenny Broughton? Oh, dear!" His had been a complicated tax return involving hours of work and Mr Pringle needed to know if his bank account had been credited with seventy-six pounds. He hurried along the pavement, pushed his plastic into the hole in the wall, tapped out his request and waited confidently for the microchip to obey.

Immediately the plate-glass shutter slid down and behind it, OPEN switched to CLOSED. Mr Pringle was affronted. He tugged but the shutter wouldn't budge. His fingers scrabbled against the glass. All at once the frustration of being both sixty-five and a *nouveau pauvre* overcame him. Stepping back, he raised his umbrella and thwacked the shutter with all his might.

The microchip retaliated, regurgitatively. The shutter lifted a fraction so that he might hear the sound and through the slit, extruded plastic shards fluttered down. Above, in pointillist red dots, a message confirmed that Mr Pringle's request had been cancelled.

He made his way despondently down John Prince's Street. Uneasiness about Ashley Fallowfield returned as he battled his way across Oxford Circus, using his ferrule to push aside ankle-deep filth and discarded fast-food containers. Not only was he bereft of his essential piece of plastic, but increasing age made London appear threatening as well as shabby. Surely people used not to scowl so much?

Soho wasn't an area familiar to him, but Mr Pringle knew of its reputation. It didn't surprise him to see photographers or police vehicles. He was more fascinated by a group of traffic wardens busily clamping a Rolls Royce, and stopped to watch. It was refreshing to see people enjoying their work for a change. He raised his hat to a jolly West Indian lady sellotaping a DON'T PANIC notice on to the windscreen. "Excuse me . . . I'm looking for Rainbow Television?"

She jerked a thumb. "If this belongs to them, you can break the good news, darlin'." He noticed for the first time that one of the entrances opposite had a multi-coloured arch. Skirting an anonymous van with its doors wide open, Mr Pringle mounted the steps.

There were uniformed men in the foyer and one of them spoke to him, but he wasn't to be caught that easily. This was a factory of make-believe. He'd been in a TV studios once before and knew that people wearing uniforms were never real; they were actors. Turning a deaf ear, Mr Pringle looked about and saw double doors labelled STUDIO: QUIET PLEASE swing open. My goodness, they must be about to film a scene. Was this what was known as a rehearsal?

Three men emerged, two of them wheeling a six foot trolley on which there was a long, green plastic bag. Mr Pringle was looking round to see where the TV camera might be hidden, when the third man stopped abruptly. "Who let him in?" demanded DS Mullin of one of the constables, but Mr Pringle had spotted a familiar figure descending the stairs beside the lift.

"Mr Fallowfield, I believe?" He hesitated because the hair was so much more golden than memory, and was brought up short by the trolley which now blocked his path. He tried again, "It is Mr Fallowfield, isn't it?" Curiously, Ashley stayed where he was, on the bottom stair, but Mr Pringle recognized him clearly now. He transferred umbrella and attaché case, resting them on the trolley, as he leaned over and stretched out his hand. "G D H Pringle. Nice to see you again. I apologize for being a little late."

They were staring at his umbrella. Too late Mr Pringle saw the remains of a hamburger embedded on the tip. "Dear me, I am sorry." He looked round for a waste basket and finding none, his hand strayed toward the green bag. "Is this intended for rubbish?"

"I shouldn't, if I were you, harte," Ashley said quickly. "Not quite Margarite's style. She was more of a gardenia person."

Perhaps because none could think of an apposite phrase, no one spoke. Mr Pringle could feel the cold metal of the trolley frame through his trouser legs. The bag was directly beneath his nose. He became acutely aware of its length, width, dull olive surface and the nature of the object which it probably contained. Ashley stepped into the social breach.

"Margarite Pelouse. I don't know whether you and she ever . . . ?" Mr Pringle wanted to say that he hadn't had the pleasure, but his tongue cleaved to the roof of his mouth. "Someone stuck a knife in her this morning. It's been one of those days, I'm afraid."

The world spun round in front of his eyes; he wanted to escape but his heart was thumping so fast he couldn't even move. The hand clutching the attaché case gave a convulsive tremor, and Mr Pringle fainted.

Studio A. Wardrobe room

The wardrobe room was overfull, divided into small changing areas by rails of costumes. A work table stood against a mirrored wall and reflected the two women who faced one another.

DPW Sylvia Mackenzie had encountered enough prejudice for one lifetime: her choice of career hadn't been an easy option. She'd learned to put up with male colleagues' unsubtle sexual innuendo. She'd also discovered among some of the higher ranks, calcified minds still classified women with blacks and deviants —so what? Wasn't this what feminism was all about? The thought stiffened her resolve. She intended to become a commander before she was through, without losing her femininity, either. She'd been born with that, she saw no reason to scorn it.

She wondered briefly if the woman in front of her had ever considered herself in similar terms. If so, why had she not begun by improving on nature? Apart from being ugly, Rita Phelps was a damn difficult witness as well.

Rita, a former dresser, now wardrobe mistress at Rainbow Television, stood her ground and held on to one of the anaesthetist's gowns. Dark, wiry, with a splay of teeth that could uncap a bottle, she'd nothing but contempt for authority, especially women who pretended to be policemen.

"I don't care, I'm not saying another word till I see whoever's in charge — and this costume does not leave Wardrobe without my say-so."

"Don't handle it!" DPW Mackenzie yelped. "Give Forensic a chance."

"Forensic . . ." Rita's contempt expanded to include every laboratory in the land. "They've made mistakes in their time. As for Margarite, good riddance, that's what I say. I knew her when she was on the boards. She might have been Tennants' blue-eyed leading lady, but her dresser had a dog's life. Never a tip no matter how well the show was doing."

"Look, I'll see if Detective Inspector Newton is free —"

"You do that. And this . . ." Rita waggled the garment under her nose, "stays here."

30

At least she'll keep it safe, DPW Mackenzie thought angrily. She had to hurry to keep up with Newton on the way back. As they turned a corner they almost collided with Ashley, supporting a sickly-looking, mousy-haired elderly gent with a moustache and wearing spectacles.

"Take a good look, harte," Ashley announced quickly. "These two are real. You can tell because the man's not wearing make-up." This was *sotto* but not *sotto* enough. He introduced his companion gaily, "Meet Mr G B H, my financial adviser."

"G *D* H," said Mr Pringle weakly, "Pringle."

"Can't stop just now, sir. We'll catch up with one another later."

Another of Ashley's confidential asides reached DI Newton as he strode away. "That one's ever so shy. He's always running away," making him grind his teeth. Sylvia Mackenzie thought it prudent to continue as though she hadn't heard.

"According to Mrs Phelps, costumes are kept in the studio wardrobe room on recording days rather than the dressing rooms. There are two rails, one for the regular cast's garments and one for Extras, but when I asked which this gown belonged to, she refused to answer."

"I want it bagged for the Lab. Go and tell George."

"Yes, sir." The policewoman disappeared. DI Newton put on a genial expression, and entered.

"Mrs Phelps? I understand you've something to show me." Rita's upper lid lifted to reveal more of her gum. DI Newton recognized this as a smile, and responded.

"Are you the one in charge then?"

"I am," he said pleasantly.

"My nephew joined the police, for the money. Bent as a hairpin . . ." A pulse, unknown until today, began to throb in DI Newton's temple.

"Is this the gown? Someone's been tampering with it, I gather?"

"It's got blood all over it, don't know whether you'd call that tampering." Rita spread it over the table top. The reddish brown blotches were already stiff. "Soaked, more like. That never came from a Leichner bottle." DI Newton agreed.

31

"We shall have to take your prints as you've been handling it."

"I've been preventing whoever it was from coming back and nicking it." Rita Phelps was indignant.

"Where did you find it?"

She pointed to the wide calico-sided container drum. "That's where they put costumes for washing, only I always sort 'em and put those that aren't too bad back on the rails. Detergent weakens the fabric and you never know, we might be doing another series. I was in 'ere lunchtime to prevent anyone going out of 'ere wearing one of 'em," Rita said righteously. "When I heard Robert yelling his head off, I looked up there," she indicated the TV monitor high on the wall. "You could see the handle of the knife. Make-up won't half cop it, I said. We all thought it was one of Margarite's jokes, you see. Wicked, she could be at times."

"Was this particular costume due to be worn today?"

"No. We do any operating scenes first thing Tuesdays, not on Mondays. One of the extras had a gown and a mask for the corridor scene, only he put his back." She pointed to another green garment among the massed blue of the nurses' uniforms.

"So who normally wears this one?"

"Dr Watkins. It's got his name in the neck." Rita's top gum was exposed in another leer. "In other words, Ian Walsh."

Programme controller's office

"It's maddening when you consider, harte; this place is full of nurses and none of them's the slightest bit of use if you're feeling poorly. The security man keeps a bottle of aspirin but that's your lot . . . here, have a sip of this." He clasped Mr Pringle's trembling fingers round the glass of water. "You're ever such a funny colour — you sure you don't want a proper doctor?"

"Just a few minutes more . . ." Mr Pringle closed his eyes.

"Take as long as you like. Sorry I had to break the news like that, but I was terrified you'd undo that zip. How about a brandy? The head of Creativity has everything under the sun in his drinks cabinet."

"A cup of tea would be nice."

"Ah, that could be tricky, but I'll try." Ashley opened the door of the secretary's office, "Angela, any chance of a cuppa, doll? As a favour?"

"Hmm!"

"Bloody women's libbers," he muttered on his return. "My regular girl's on holiday. This one's a temp from a women's co-operative in Camden Passage. It needs a democratic decision before she'll even fill the kettle. Listen, if you'd rather go home and rest? Come back another day . . . ?" Mr Pringle opened one eye. The patch of sky above the rooftops was pregnant with rain.

"I'd prefer to begin as soon as possible."

"Oh, well then." Ashley produced from under his desk a Harrods carrier bag, brimful. "The taxman's been sending me these billets-doux for years and now he says he won't take no for an answer."

Studio A. Prop store/interview room

The property master had responded to a request for a witness's chair with a medieval throne complete with tapestry upholstery and gilded carved arms. If DI Newton thought witnesses might find it too grand, he was wrong. He'd overlooked the fact that most were actors. All the same, Ian Walsh looked nervous sitting there. Newton couldn't fathom why. Perhaps Walsh found the solid hulk of DS Mullin oppressive.

From behind the desk, Frank Newton watched as much as he listened. Walsh seemed unduly perturbed when told that one of his costumes had been used by the killer. The choice of garment wasn't surprising — a gown's voluminous folds gave protection as well as anonymity — it was bound to belong to someone in the cast. All it proved as far as the inspector was concerned was that the attack had been premeditated.

There was silence. Ian Walsh had finished speaking. Newton roused himself. "Thank you very much, sir. Most helpful." He looked at Mullin. "Any more questions you'd like to ask?" The sergeant saw it as an opportunity to shine but for Newton, it was yet another chance to let information flow over him and absorb the actor's body language.

How old was Walsh, late twenties? Tanned like one or two in

33

the cast. Probably took good care of himself. An actor needed to be fit and supple. Over-smart in his shirt and tie — presumably for his part as Dr Watkins? In a pause the inspector interrupted to ask, and Walsh confirmed it.

"Bernard suggested we remain in costume so that if there was the slightest chance of recording a few more scenes . . ."

"Not today. Tomorrow perhaps."

"Oh, well." Ian Walsh gave a graceful shrug. "We owe it to Margarite." Newton took up the point.

"There have been suggestions that Miss Pelouse wasn't a popular member of the cast?" Ian Walsh picked his way through a potential minefield.

"She had been a big star."

"So I understand."

"Not so well known to audiences nowadays," and he paused.

"I should've thought your particular viewing public knew her well enough?" Newton felt sure the business consortium had them accurately targeted.

"That's true," Ian Walsh agreed, "but Margarite was used to bigger things, not a soap opera. I think that's what made her — difficult." Newton tried a different tack.

"I'm told she had a reputation as a practical joker?" This produced a reaction: Walsh reddened under the tan.

"I don't think she always understood the devastating effect some of her pranks had."

"Anything happen to you?" Walsh remained silent. "In confidence, Mr Walsh. Whatever you say will remain within these walls." But it was Walsh's gown the killer had worn.

"After I've spoken to a solicitor," he mumbled.

"Oh come, sir, no need to be alarmed. We *know* it couldn't have been you. What chump would put on his own costume before killing the old lady and then put it in the laundry basket for Mrs Phelps to find —"

"Is that where it was?" Ian sounded genuinely surprised. "When it wasn't in my dressing room this morning, I asked my dresser to find it or get me another." Detective Inspector Newton looked at him more attentively.

"You didn't mention that before, Mr Walsh? I was given to

understand all the costumes were kept in the studio wardrobe room." The actor was annoyed.

"If Rita had her way, you mean? She's a lazy slut. If it were left to her we'd have filthy costumes week after week. Thank God for dressers like Henry. He knows I don't want to wear someone else's sweaty left-overs. How can one give a performance —"

"Henry . . . ?"

"Titmouse. Marvellous old man. Worked in the West End all his life, still does if he gets the chance. First thing every Monday morning he and I check my clothes for the week. Once that's done, I can relax and concentrate on building up my character." DI Newton knew this must be to do with acting and lost interest.

"One vital question, Mr Walsh. Have *you* any idea why anyone should want to kill Miss Pelouse?" Ian Walsh's gaze was untroubled. Perhaps his voice was a little too emphatic but he didn't hesitate.

"None whatsoever."

Male extras' dressing room
Non-speaking artistes, divided by sex, occupied two long, narrow rooms at the end of the dressing room corridor. Today, twelve of them crowded into one room, seeking comfort. Out of habit, whether sitting on chairs or the bench along the wall, they all faced the brightly lit mirrors as they conversed with one another. The noise was that of a pigeon loft, billing and cooing as they speculated and wove fantasies to fill the time.

"It was in my horoscope this morning . . . Here we are: 'Avoid any unpleasantness on the 8th'. If only one had paid attention! 'Lucky birthday, Friday 12th'."

"Is yours on the 12th, Iris?"

"No."

"I think Margarite was Libra."

"It says: 'Storm clouds lie ahead' for Librans. I'm Gemini."

"D'you think they'll let us go soon?"

"When they've talked to us, that's what the lady policeman said."

"I didn't see Miss Charles, I wasn't near the set. I told them so straight away."

"Did you mention Jacinta Charles by name?" Eleven pairs of eyes stared at the betrayer accusingly.

"Of course I didn't! I don't blame her and I shan't let her down."

"We don't know for certain it was her."

"We all read *The Stage*, Daphne. How could it have been anyone else?"

"Oh, God . . . I'm sorry — please excuse me!" The one who stumbled outside was a handsome, silvery-haired man. There was silence for a moment or two. One of the younger women mouthed the word "drunk" to her neighbour and was spotted.

"Mr Bowman is taking it hard, as one would expect," Iris, the female doyenne reproached. "Apart from his natural sensitivity, I believe he had once worked with Margarite Pelouse."

"Did you know her in the old days, Iris?"

Iris did not, so wisely made no reply. Instead she shook her head gravely to indicate profound sorrow.

"The lady policeman asked me if I knew she'd been killed *before* I went to lunch. I told her, no."

"None of us did, dear. We were all in the corridor scene."

"Iris and Beryl weren't, were you?" This time Iris fixed the questioner with a threatening stare.

"We had been told we weren't required. As is customary, I waited on the premises until the actual time of the lunchbreak." She turned to the unfortunate Beryl, "I was alone."

"I'd already gone," Beryl confessed, "I knew they wouldn't need me for the scene with Margarite and I wanted to go to Marks & Spencer."

"They might have required a cross-over, Beryl."

The hapless Beryl stared. "You surely don't think I had anything to do with . . . ?" She was saved by the soothsayer.

"I *sensed* something was wrong. I didn't actually hear Robert scream, but the vibes were dreadful in that studio this morning."

The door opened and Bertie reappeared. They made room, murmuring sympathetically.

"I told you before, what you need is a brandy, Mr Bowman," Iris said authoritatively. He shook his head in irritation. Beryl changed the subject tactfully.

"He's a lovely floor manager, isn't he, Robert? Of all of them, he's the nicest."

"And fair. He doesn't have any favourites."

"Not like some! Have you ever worked with Malcolm? He's a proper little tyrant: 'Do this, do that — don't argue.' I said to him one day, I said, 'We all have feelings, you know. We may not be real artistes but we do have our feelings.'"

"Quite right."

"Some of us *were* real artistes in our day, Beryl. If styles have changed that is hardly our fault! *I* was billed above the title more than once at Frinton on Sea." Ruffled feathers had to be allowed time to settle. There was a pause before someone asked, "Are you called tomorrow, Daphne?"

"We all are, aren't we? The agency said it was two days for everyone."

"I hope they're not going to do any operating scenes."

"Oh God, not more blood!"

Programme controller's office

Mr Pringle had recovered sufficiently. Ashley arranged a table and chair beside the window and Mr Pringle accepted an unwanted flower arrangement as well because he recognized it was well meant.

The sight of so many familiar documents was a benison to his nerves. He murmured half-forgotten identifications as he delved into the carrier and sorted them into piles. Occasionally he stopped to admire the audacity. "Ignored a P. 142/0875/13 dated June 1983 did we . . . ?" but before long the only sound from his corner of the room was pen on paper as he began his travail.

There were occasional interruptions, the first when the liberated woman from Camden marched in with new script pages.

"Richard's rewrites," she announced and withdrew. Ashley scanned them quickly.

"He's a fantastic editor. Listen to this: he's redone the storyline so that Margarite was knifed by the driver of the car *after* he'd accidentally knocked her over, because she reminded him of his dead mother whom he hated, but nobody notices the wound in Casualty when they examine her. Brilliant! Richard never fails . . ." Ashley waved the pages, "and he never misses his regular train back to Pett's Wood. Not many writers can pull out the stops in record time like that." Mr Pringle was impressed. Ashley was already dialling Bernard's number.

"Richard's produced a miracle, petal. An explanatory scene between Dr Falconer and Nurse Riddle — in the sluice room as per usual — and we'll have to recall that stunt driver. D'you think he can manage a couple of lines?" There was a long apologetic reply. Mr Pringle gathered that Bernard had doubts.

"If he's that bad, shoot him back to camera and put it right at the dub, OK?" Ashley counselled. "By the bye . . ." He became overly casual, "Let's reschedule all Jacinta's material first thing in the morning . . . I agree. Sooner or later they're bound to find out so we'll get all her scenes safely in the can as soon as poss." He hung up and pressed the intercom button. "Angela, you can photostat these and circulate them. Any news of Sherlock and Co?"

"They're going to look in when they've finished. I ought to leave in about five minutes, Mr Fallowfield. The child-minder goes at five thirty."

"Yes, yes . . ." Ashley released the button, "Come back, Barbara, you great big ugly virgin. Now, where was I?" He searched among his papers, "You all right, harte? Think you can sort things out?"

"Eventually, yes." But that wasn't what Ashley meant.

"What I really need to know is, will I have to trade down the Audi?"

"Tax avoidance is one thing, Fallowfield. Evasion is another matter altogether." Ashley's eyes were round with innocence.

"I'm not asking you to break the law, G B H —"

"I'm very glad to hear it."

"But there must be something I'm entitled to? For instance . . ." He warmed to his task, "Why can't I have a married man's allowance?" Mr Pringle looked up, startled.

"But of course you can. Forgive me, I had no idea —"

"John and I have been together for seven years. That must count for something?"

"Ah. I foresee a difficulty there."

"Narrow-minded bigots!"

"I'm so sorry. It is, on the face of it, unfair —"

"Can't you think of anything? Some little claim or other?"
Mr Pringle pondered.

"How close was your relationship with Miss Pelouse?"

"I loathed the bitch," Ashley said passionately. "D'you know,
she once made me look a fool in front of a packed house at Drury
Lane —"

"Under certain circumstances," Mr Pringle interrupted desperately, "a small percentage of the cost of mourning could be
considered tax deductible." In an instant Ashley's eyes were full
of tears.

"A magnificent artiste . . . plucked from this world, thrust into
the next."

"Quite so." The eulogy made Mr Pringle equally uneasy but
Ashley was busily assessing his wardrobe.

"How about black boxer shorts? I need new underwear before
I go on my hols."

Gradually, throughout the building, people were told they were
free to go. They hurried outside into the drizzle, trying not to
look glad. Jason Cornish was given a final shake-up by Mullin,
who watched him depart with some regret. If he'd had his way,
Cornish would have been pulled in for further questioning, but
he had to agree with Newton when challenged: on the evidence,
Cornish was the last person to want Pelouse dead.

In the shabby bedroom in Hendon, the man stared at the
ceiling and whispered his daughter's name.

Lists were being collated in the temporary studio interview
room, ready to hand to indexers back at the police station. Once
in the system, these would be cross-referenced and analysed.
Tomorrow, when the incident room was up and working, DI
Newton would allocate tasks, the most urgent one to interview
those who'd failed to return after lunch: so far two studio
technicians plus one member of the cast.

"No doubt they all have valid reasons," Newton said as he departed, "but we need to know what those are."

"Obviously. And we can begin recording again, you said?"

"Apart from using the ICU set, yes you can Mr Fallowfield."

"Marvellous. We'd finished with that set anyway, once we'd done the shot of Margarite. Do you know who killed her yet?"

"No, sir. Not many policemen are endowed with psychic powers. In my simple way I'm still trying to establish a reason for murdering her."

"Maybe someone hated her enough because of her stupid jokes?" Ashley suggested artlessly. "You heard what happened to me? Years ago we were doing a charity matinée at Drury Lane and Margarite glued my shoes to the floor. There I was, poised in the spotlight about to do a Fred Astaire routine, I went to lift my foot and fell arse over tit. *I* could've killed her then all right."

"Were most of her jokes like that?"

"Generally speaking. They were too cruel to be funny, but of course we all laughed, we were frightened of her. She used to have influence in the old days, when she was married to Alfred Barker."

"I see. Well, thank you very much, sir. We'll meet again tomorrow. Good night." Ashley waited until his footsteps died away.

"*We* know who did it, of course. By the time *they* find out, with a bit of luck, we'll have her scenes in the can." Mr Pringle stared in astonishment.

"You — know?"

"Jacinta Charles. Has to be. If he knew anything about the business he'd have charged her by now but forget I said so, OK? You're too honest. One look at your face and he'd guess you were sitting on a secret." Mr Pringle was offended. "Listen, harte, we're fifty pages behind apart from the new material, we can't afford any more interruptions." Ashley glanced at his watch. "Come on. The rain's pissing down over the yard-arm, time for a little drinkie at the Groucho and I'll tell you all about it."

3

RAW NERVES

The Newtons' living-room. Early Monday evening
It was a room that had once been elegant but hadn't withstood
the advent of one small child. Today it looked worse than usual;
there were additional fingermarks on the paintwork. Newton
knelt and began collecting scattered toys. As she watched him,
Jean rested her aching back against the door jamb.

"You knew it was her birthday party this afternoon — "

"Jean," he interrupted wearily, "I cannot fit a murder
investigation round an eight-year-old's social engagements. I
said I'd try and get back, but that's how it is. You should know
that by now." He switched on the television.

"It's not time for the news."

"I want to watch *Doctors and Nurses*. Is supper at a critical
stage or can you stay and help? I may need a bit of background on
this one."

For an officer who'd planned every stage of his career with
care, Frank Newton had married the wrong wife. Not that
anyone knew why he'd twice failed his selection board, least of
all Jean, but on each occasion she'd been going through one of
her 'difficult' spells. Unlike Mullin, Newton believed in keeping
such problems to himself. Not for him an appeal or demands for a
transfer to further his career. If it meant he'd never make chief
inspector then so be it. Surely the Gods would allow him to reach
superintendent next time round, that wasn't much to ask.

Before their marriage, Jean had been a struggling young
actress. Big eyes in a small mobile face meant she'd scraped a
living from photographic assignments and infrequent com-
mercials, but that was all. What was worse, she was fifteen years
younger than her husband. Every day some spat or other
reminded Frank Newton of that gap, but he'd only to look at her

41

to remember why he'd been so foolish: he'd fallen in love with Jean despite her capricious nature. He was still in love nine years later.

She waited impatiently as he tidied the toys before pouring them each a drink. On screen, advertisements screamed a silent message.

"How can I help, and what's murder got to do with a soap?"

"Ever heard of Margarite Pelouse?" Jean Newton laughed as she took her gin.

"Who hasn't? Thanks. One of the grand old dames of British Theatre — except that she never has been made a dame, come to think of it."

"Well, it's too late now. Someone stabbed her to death this morning."

"Good grief! Who'd do a thing like that?"

"That's what we'd dearly like to know." Jean recovered quickly.

"Why watch this thing?"

"She was about to play a part in it; as a guest patient of some description."

"The 'unknown patient'; it's the hook they use, the reason why most people switch on. Fancy Margarite Pelouse agreeing to do it — she can't have needed the money. And what a thing to happen! Well, it's no good asking me about her. I never moved in such exalted circles."

"I spoke to her current agent this afternoon, to try and fill in the background. He was cagey, apart from what was already public knowledge. As she seems to have changed agents as often as husbands, he may not have known much anyway. According to him, she was born . . ." Newton flicked through his memory, "Margarita Erika Freidburg, I think it was — precise date and place of birth unknown. He thinks she became a British citizen when she married her first husband, that's all we've discovered so far. We'll have to speak to her former agent tomorrow."

"I always imagined she was Czech or Hungarian."

"You could be right. She had British nationality and was a divorcee by the time she married the impresario, Alfred Barker.

He changed her name and made her a star. The rest, as they say, is history."

The opening titles of *Doctors and Nurses* rolled across the screen. Newton picked up the control box and joined his wife on the sofa.

"Everyone knew about her marriage to Barker and how he built her into a star," Jean raised her voice above the sugary chords. "She was a fine actress but she also had the reputation of being a menace to work with." When Frank made no comment, she said idly, "I wonder how old she was?"

"The post mortem will give an indication."

"Urgh!"

"Tell me what you know about the regular cast." Jean concentrated.

"That's Ian Walsh. He plays one of the doctors, a sort of houseman cum anaesthetist — it's amazing how flexible doctors can be in a soap! He used to be in *Coronation Street*."

"Uh-huh."

A black sister walked across the shot but didn't speak.

"I don't know her."

"She's a size fourteen." Newton grinned at his wife's expression. "What about the nurse coming on now?"

"Jacinta Charles, Nurse Williams . . ." Jean Newton stared, "Jacinta Charles, of course! It was in *The Stage*."

"What was?"

"Jacinta Charles claimed that her mother was related to Margarite Pelouse, some sort of cousin by marriage, I think."

"Why wasn't I told!" Newton was indignant. "The agent didn't say a word about that. Go on, what else do you know?"

"Jacinta Charles went to LAMDA — as a mature student, I believe. She made quite an impression as Viola in her final term — I remember reading the write-ups about five or six years ago. She's had the occasional part since, but never really got anywhere. Obviously she was hoping Margarite Pelouse would give her career a boost, but it all fizzled out. Nothing seemed to happen. Next thing, she's playing Nurse Williams in *Doctors and Nurses*."

"Not a direct route to stardom?"

43

"She'll be type-cast unless she's very lucky," Jean Newton said shrewdly. "Not many get to the top after that. In fact, I'd say she'll never make it. She's more juvenile than leading lady material, but at her age she should be moving into that category. The thing is, if her claim was true and if Margarite Pelouse had used her influence, it could've made all the difference."

"At Rainbow Television — everyone would know this?"

"They must have done. The profession read *The Stage* even if policemen don't."

He ignored the barb just as he turned a deaf ear to Jean's jealous, "Fancy you being in a TV studio? I'd have given anything to audition for that series." The fact that Frank patently wasn't listening, annoyed her further. "I may well decide to go back to the business once Emma's old enough."

"Oh, don't be so silly!" It was automatic after what he'd gone through today, but immediately Newton knew he shouldn't have said it. Jean looked tired. One gin hadn't compensated for two hours with six eight-year-olds and there was still the jelly to clean off the dining-room walls.

"Don't speak to me like that! I had a career before I married you!" Such an exaggeration made him gape and fuelled the flames. "It's bloody unfair! You have all the fun —"

"Fun!"

"While I'm stuck here! Well, I've had enough. I'm going out." She was on her feet and in the hall, grabbing her coat and bag. Despite his dismay, Newton managed to swallow an enquiry about supper.

"When will you be back?" he asked mildly.

"I've no idea!"

The front door slammed. Upstairs he could hear the throb of his daughter's new record player. He wandered into the kitchen, but it wasn't apparent what was intended so he knew he'd better wait. Back in the living-room, he poured another drink and wondered uneasily which of their neighbours Jean had chosen to confide in this evening. Later, when she returned, it would be up to him to calm her down. He'd done it before. He hoped she'd forget the whole stupid idea. If Jacinta Charles couldn't make it to stardom, Frank Newton was damned sure his wife didn't stand a chance.

On screen, the Channel 4 news began with a photograph of Margarite Pelouse as Cleopatra taken during the 1960s, her imperious bony profile outlined against black velvet curtains. Newton waited until the picture changed before pressing the sound button. Peter Sissons gazed at him implacably:

"Following on from this incident, a success rate of less than thirty per cent for solving serious crimes in the Metropolitan area has been reported today —" Frank Newton hurled the control box across the room.

Wine bar in Soho

Their exit from the studio that evening had mystified Mr Pringle. He thought they would make a discreet dash past the Press cameras. To his surprise, Ashley, who'd put on dark glasses and turned up his midnight-blue racoon collar, waited on the top step, turning this way and that, until the last of the flashlights finished crackling in the downpour.

Slightly damp himself, Mr Pringle now consumed a second glass of acidic red and listened as his employer expounded.

"I knew there might be trouble as soon as I told Jacinta that Margarite was coming in as replacement, I could see it in her face. Yesterday, there was a bit of a row apparently, but Jason Cornish arrived on the scene and nothing much was said after that. I get all the gossip from Alix, the stage-manager. I need to hear about these minor crises, to nip them in the bud. I didn't realize things were so serious. *Why* Jacinta took it in her head to stick a knife in this morning, God alone knows . . ." Ashley shrugged padded shoulders, "That's between her and the police when she decides to confess, but it has solved another of my little problems."

"Which one's that?"

"There are too many regulars," Ashley said simply. "From time to time we have to weed in order to introduce fresh faces. How, is always a difficulty. One wants to be kind. In one soap they filled a coach with half the cast and had it crash on the motorway."

"You could have someone announce that Nurse Williams has been arrested for murder?"

"Not terribly subtle, harte," Ashley looked pained. "I thought Dr Watkins could find a farewell note in his locker — give Ian a chance to do face acting. He's awfully good you know. Then we'll have him on the phone — you won't hear the other voice — pleading with Nurse Williams to return for the sake of her patients."

"But she won't."

"Not for seven years or so, no. We could hear of her sacrificing herself by going to an NHS hospital? Yes, that would be a nice touch. It'll remind the viewers Jacinta's in prison. Her fans might write and cheer her up. What d'you think?"

"It seems such a ferocious method for a woman to choose . . ." Mr Pringle couldn't rid himself of the image of the killing. "And why kill a relative out of disappointment — I find that difficult to believe."

"Lizzie Borden did. Don't forget, harte, Jacinta's a strong, healthy girl and those medical knives are frightfully sharp. We bought them second-hand from an NHS hospital closed by the cuts. All the same, I should never have brought Margarite into the cast." Ashley sighed. "It was too tempting. I guessed we might attract publicity. I was thinking of the ratings of course."

"Oh, look," Mr Pringle was staring at the TV monitor behind the bar. "There's a picture of Miss Pelouse. Oh my goodness, there's you!"

Ashley examined his image dispassionately. "The wrong profile . . . and I'm overdue for a rinse." He patted the curls, signalled for more drinks and repeated, "I never expected Jacinta to go berserk."

"Perhaps she didn't?"

"Oh, it must've been her. Otherwise it has to be one of the others." Ashley didn't want to think about that. All of them were due at the studio tomorrow.

"You will tell the police all that you've told me about Miss Charles?"

"After we've recorded the last of Jacinta's scenes. Richard's a marvel, but even he couldn't rewrite this episode a third time. The trouble is, everyone on the site knows — I hope to God none of them spill the beans to dear old Sergeant Cork."

"You can rely on my discretion," Mr Pringle said solemnly. A third glass had appeared and he wondered if he dared. "I shall be as silent as the gr . . . I shall not speak of it."

Very small bedsit in Covent Garden

In the estate agent's brochure, it had been described as a *pied-à-terre*. Jacinta Charles had stowed most of her possessions on shelves or under the sofa-bed, but even so there was very little room. It was Simon's joke that only one person could get dressed at a time — Simon! Despite what had happened, her heart ached for him. His voice over the phone was unfamiliarly querulous and made her even more nervous.

"But you know I'm innocent so why are you trying to avoid me?" At his end, under a plastic dome at Tottenham Court station, the young cameraman mumbled something.

"I can't hear you!" she cried impatiently.

"I said, we'll have to be discreet. Until the whole thing's blown over."

"Oh, don't be stupid. If everyone sees you backing off, it'll confirm their worst suspicions."

"Jacy, I can't risk my wife finding out, not just yet."

"Oh, so that's it." Jacinta's voice was bleak. Immediately, Simon tried to shift the blame from himself.

"Don't start jumping to conclusions, Jacy. It's just that this whole thing . . . I mean, it's so unexpected . . . and there's bound to be adverse publicity . . . anyone, however remotely connected with Margarite —"

"You want to pull out. That's the truth, isn't it? What's happened has provided you with the perfect excuse."

"No . . . not exactly." Another fact, even more stark, had to be faced and Jacinta Charles cried out in agonized disbelief.

"You think I did it! You don't believe I'm innocent!" She didn't wait for his reply but crashed down the receiver and sat staring blankly at the opposite wall. All of a sudden, she shivered.

The Bricklayers. Saloon bar

Monday was the quietest night of the week and therefore the one on which Mavis Bignell enjoyed her work as a part-time barmaid most. It was also one of the nights when Mr Pringle visited just before closing time in order to accompany her home, a reason that made her brisk with stragglers.

It didn't take more than minutes to check the till, drape her tea-cloth over the pumps and call farewell to the landlord. Mr Pringle took down her coat, warmed it in front of the fire and held it out for her.

"Ta, dear. Chilly out?"

"Damp."

"Did you remember your long johns this morning?" It wasn't a wish to cool his ardour, he knew, but a loving concern for his well-being. He thanked her politely. Once they were safely outside however, where walls no longer had ears, she looked at him closely.

"Now then, what's all this it said on the news about that actress being killed."

"I fear she was, yes."

"I don't want you going back there then, not until they've found out who did it. It might not be safe."

"Mavis, I cannot let Fallowfield down, his business affairs are in a shocking state. And whatever you heard, you need have no fears about my safety. The identity of the culprit appears to be common knowledge. It can only be a matter of time before the police discover it for themselves."

"Hmm." Mrs Bignell was only half convinced, but walked along in silence for a while.

Over the years the two of them had established a routine which combined satisfactorily a desire for companionship as well as for privacy. Mrs Bignall had been heard to declare at the beginning that she'd been swept off her feet, adding contentedly there was nothing quite like it.

As for Mr Pringle, he'd been very lonely when they first met. Grieving for Renée had faded into the realization that there was no one with whom to share the rest of his life. Retirement stretched into limitless emptiness until he encountered Mavis, naked, deputizing as the model for "Beginners in Oils".

A shy man, Mr Pringle had been overcome by her exuberant figure and Titian hair. That night a demoniac energy inspired him. He'd slapped on paint like one possessed — as indeed he was — and at the finish, Mavis declared the thickly coated canvas "a masterpiece".

He'd put away his paints and sold his easel after that; the course had more than fulfilled its purpose. That night the model had stepped down from her dais and filled the void in his life to their mutual satisfaction.

So it came about that on certain days Mrs Bignell would visit Mr Pringle; on others, he would stay with her. He had offered matrimony several times, but Mavis was steadfast in her determination to preserve the romance in their relationship.

Tonight, holding his arm tightly, she insisted, "I still think you should tell Mr Fallowfield you don't want to sort out his tax until it's settled."

"If Fallowfield is correct, the whole business will probably be resolved by tomorrow."

In her warm, comfortable kitchen they discussed it again over their cocoa. "You're sure there's no risk?"

"Fallowfield has installed me in a corner of his office. Outside there is a stalwart young woman who protects us both."

Mavis was unconvinced.

"It was a woman who was responsible for killing Margarite Pelouse, according to you."

"Remember that was in confidence, Mavis. Although Fallowfield seemed certain, the only evidence against Miss Charles appears to be a grudge that her relationship with Miss Pelouse hadn't been acknowledged."

"Promise me you won't get involved." Mr Pringle had a flash of memory, of the dark, olive green bag and clutched his mug in a sudden cold spasm.

"I shall take every precaution."

"Have a ginger-nut," said Mavis. She didn't reproach him when he dunked it; there were occasions when one ignored a lapse.

"How long before you've earned enough for your new roof?" she asked.

"Ah, I've had a stroke of luck there. Fallowfield has offered additional work, checking employees' expense sheets. Some of the claims are completely unacceptable to the Revenue and I've agreed to explain why to the people concerned." Mavis looked grim.

"Promise me you won't sit with your back to a door all the time you're there."

"After tomorrow, the murderer should be under lock and key."

"It wasn't her I was thinking of."

4

CASUALTY!

Studio A. Make-up room. Tuesday morning

The atmosphere in any television make-up room is carefully contrived; warm, womblike and peaceful, designed to soothe away stage fright. Rainbow's was no exception, even if the décor was excessively pink. The chairs were comfortable, there was every inducement to relax, but Jacinta Charles was taut. She lit her third cigarette watched by the vapid young girl smoothing on cleanser.

"I thought you'd given up?" The question was over-bright.

"So did I." Jacinta's gaze remained level but the girl's eyes dropped as she busied herself with cottonwool and skin tonic. "I didn't do it, Tracy," Jacinta said softly. "It wasn't me who killed Margarite."

"No." There was disbelief in that syllable. Jacinta stubbed out the cigarette. All the effort it had taken to get out of bed and come here this morning instead of running away . . She said loudly and defiantly:

"When I've finished today, I'm going to tell the police everything. So that they can cross me off the list and get on with discovering who really did it. And when I come back, Tracy, if you don't apologize, I might actually stick a knife in your gullet to see how you react." Brushes and jars scattered as the girl screamed. Round the room, in front of other mirrors, artistes jerked upright. The supervisor came hurrying across.

"Anything wrong?"

"Yes." Jacinta turned to face her. "Do you believe I did it, Jo?" This time there was no hesitation.

"No, I don't. It's the silliest suggestion I've ever heard."

"Then would you mind finishing me off?" The brave front was beginning to crack. Jacinta gripped the arm of her chair. "I just can't stand people who think . . ."

"Don't worry." The supervisor gave an eloquent look and Tracy sulked away. "That stupid little madam can wash the powder puffs for a change." Jo smoothed on foundation cream. "What colours are you wearing today?"

"Just make sure the mascara's waterproof."

"OK." Fingers smoothed and patted like butterflies. "How's Simon taking it?"

"He's gone back to his wife."

"Oh." The two women looked briefly at one another. "I think you're about to discover who your friends are, Jacy."

"I think I already have."

Police station. Incident room
It was a functional room with windows at one end. Walls and ceiling were acoustically panelled and clean, but the scuffed carpet tiles were marked with ancient coffee stains. Two Holmes computer terminals stood back to back on a corner table, idle while their operators waited for information. Desks and metal filing cabinets lined three sides of the room, but in pride of place in the centre was the table containing twin carousels fed by two young indexers.

The office manager, DS Wicander, chose to ignore their chatter as they slotted in the completed multi-coloured reference cards. However irritating, both girls could combine an in-depth discussion on eye-shadow with accurate filing.

Wicander had been moved sideways on this occasion to allow for Mullin's secondment. Outwardly he maintained his tubby, cheerful persona, concealing irritation, but like Newton he felt it was an unnecessary disruption. Theirs was a smooth-running team. However, look on the bright side, there were compensations; it was lousy weather and here he was at a desk with a radiator warming his back. Wicander stretched voluptuously and contemplated his second doughnut of the morning. His receiver, Edwards, examined the allocation board on the wall, debating how best to distribute the first Actions of the day.

"Give 'em all to Mullin," Wicander suggested without being asked.

"He's got plenty already."

"So? He wants to prove how good he is. Give the lad his head, mate." Wicander's bonhomie compensated, as he saw it, for Newton's silences. Normally Edwards was office manager, but he too had been shifted. He was finding Wicander's suggestions increasingly annoying. Against his judgment he picked up the pentel; anything for a quiet life.

"As a way of getting rid, you mean?"

"Too right!" Wicander was emphatic. Edwards added three more numbers to the white square beside Mullin's name.

"Better not overdo it, Doreen can help," he gave her the final two Actions and entered their names on the sheets.

Around the room, members of the team double-checked names and addresses before passing completed cards to the computer operators who entered the information and returned them to the indexers.

Every person at Rainbow Television had to be accounted for, plus his or her vehicle registration, written in reverse. If one of these numbers became relevant for any reason, it was the last few digits witnesses usually remembered.

Once a suspect came under scrutiny, their card would be duplicated and cross-referenced, checked against the Criminal Records Office as well as the Swansea computer. It was painstaking, time-consuming work, designed to prevent a single relevant fact slipping unnoticed through the net. Belt and braces, as Frank Newton was the first to admit.

He trusted the carousel system. It fitted in with his methodical approach. He liked to handle the cards, to reread any comments his team members made. Because he knew the men and women who made them, he could sometimes read between the words.

The Holmes system was a Godsend once they needed to compare facts or pull out information, but at this stage, each card represented a person; another face in the crowd who'd sur-rounded Margarite Pelouse. Frank Newton wanted to get to know them personally.

"Right . . . Morning everyone, let's have a meeting." Newton looked bilious. His team recognized familiar symptoms. The boss had obviously had a bad night, presumably because his wife was up to her tricks again. They never had much to go on,

Newton never divulged a thing, but as a team they were accustomed to reaching conclusions from the minimum of facts. It was going to be, Wicander decided, a "let's get at it" day. He regarded his boss as a cold fish. DPW Mackenzie was more loyal.

"These Actions relating to theatrical agents, d'you want statements from any of them, Frank?"

"I don't think so, not at this stage. It's the recent background that's important, also whether the deceased had any connection with the rest of the cast, in particular Jacinta Charles." Newton gave her the bones of Jean's story; it was up to Sylvia Mackenzie to dig out the facts and check. A newspaper article might turn out to be nothing more than unfounded gossip.

"Understood."

"About this Miss Charles, Guv —"

"Names and addresses of those at the studio we didn't see yesterday first, Mullin. You can assist Doreen."

"Yes, Guv."

Newton didn't yet know whether he was reliable — and when would someone tell the burk not to use that word!

"Who took Henry Titmouse's details? He's one of their dressers." A hand went up. "I want to know when Titmouse last saw or handled that anaesthetist's gown. Also anything else he can remember about it."

"Sir."

"The stage-manager . . . Alix Baxter? Has George filed his Exhibits report? I want to know if that breast knife was in her cage when she unlocked it yesterday morning."

The investigation had moved into gear. Frank Newton was grateful he could apply the balm of routine to mental as well as physical symptoms. It had become more and more of a habit lately. There was a twinge of guilt — this was what Jean meant when she talked of "fun" — he could escape but she was stuck. He'd tentatively suggested part-time work, but she'd been scornful. An office — any office — would be exchanging one prison for another, he was informed. Didn't he realize what that could do to someone with an artistic temperament?

Newton switched his mind back to the present. No doubt he'd have his full of histrionics in this case with all the thespians

54

involved. And there were other statements waiting to be checked, relating to the drug pusher's death fall last week. He finished the briefing at double speed. "Next meeting, four o'clock this afternoon. Right then, let's get at it."

A street in W1. Morning rush hour
Mr Pringle forced his way across to the inside of the pavement. Frantic commuters continued to sweep him along Oxford Street, but in a few more yards he needed to turn right.

It was unnecessarily early, but he was keen to return to his paperwork. Yesterday he'd been stimulated by the sight of memos involving so many districts of the Revenue. Fallowfield's haphazard career had involved a criss-crossing of manilla folders throughout England and Wales. How wonderful linked terminals must be now compared to the tedious internal mailing system Mr Pringle had known. But those same folders had also revived half-forgotten memories, of a desire to succeed when it came to unravelling a mess.

He paused to inhale the wild perfume of a London meadow: exhaust gases mingled with rotting black bags of garbage left outside offices the night before. He reached his turning and broke free of the surging human maelstrom.

In quieter Soho backwaters Mr Pringle analysed his change of mood. Why was he buoyant all of a sudden? Since he'd advertised his services, people had come with their problems and thanked him for the results — albeit with grudging resignation on occasion. He put his finger on it: the absence of a feeling of pressure, that was it. For the first time in years, Mr Pringle had the satisfaction of working at his own pace. Perhaps senior citizenship conferred advantages after all?

Hurrying ahead of him towards the studios were one or two he recognized from yesterday. He loitered, not wishing to arrive when the receptionist was busy with dressing room keys. Besides, there was another experience to savour today. He was due to be issued with a temporary staff pass and that meant having his photograph taken. If it turned out to be flattering, he would beg a copy for Mrs Bignell. He wondered if he also dare request a sprucing-up session first. Once, at Bath & Wells

Television, a make-up lady had given him a trim, shampoo and set. Mr Pringle recalled it as a most enjoyable experience, especially when Mavis demonstrated her appreciation afterwards.

A car paused close to where the Rolls had been clamped the day before. The driver was scrutinizing buildings, as if searching for an address. Mr Pringle looked round anxiously for the traffic warden; ought he to warn the driver?

Those heading for the studios were crossing the road ahead when the car pulled away from the kerb abruptly as if the driver now realized he was in the wrong location altogether. One of the pedestrians obviously hadn't noticed, but there wasn't time to shout a warning. At the last second the man spun round and saw the car. He made no attempt to save himself. Terror seemed to paralyse him, as it did Mr Pringle. The impact of the collision lifted the man bodily and he twisted in mid-air, as if to avoid the wheels, but wasn't agile enough. He fell heavily, crushed by both rear tyres.

It was the agonized scream which finally released Mr Pringle from his trance. Speeding away, apparently oblivious, the car continued steadily, disappearing from sight round a corner.

On shaky, uncertain legs Mr Pringle staggered forward and knelt beside the heap in the road. The man moved once, convulsively, and groaned. Mr Pringle remembered vaguely there were many things he ought to be doing but could recall none of them. Instead he put an arm under the man's head and when this seemed to ease him, slid the man's carrier bag underneath to act as a pillow.

It had all happened so quickly. One moment Mr Pringle had been enjoying the prospect of the day ahead, now he was gazing down at a face contorted with pain.

"Oh . . . God!"

"Hang on, old chap. Help is on its way." Full of doubt, Mr Pringle looked round wildly at the crowd who'd gathered from nowhere. "Has anyone sent for an ambulance?"

"A geezer's gone to find a phone."

"Is there a doctor . . . or a nurse?" This time they were silent. He noticed something; the sleeve that had been beneath the victim was soaked with blood. There must be a wound at the back of the skull. As calmly as he could, Mr Pringle said quietly, "Can you manage to lie completely still. It would be best if you could." The mane of silvery hair didn't move but the eyes looked up at him.

"Not to blame . . . my fault," the man murmured, perfectly lucidly.

His words were a trigger for the crowd who up till now had simply shoved or stood on tiptoe to get a better view. Various opinions burst forth with one voice topping the rest: "And I got his number!"

"Write it down, then," Mr Pringle ordered. "There's my newspaper, use that." He glanced again at the victim who had his eyes closed against their arguments. The mouth was a sharp, pallid line of pain. "Hang on," Mr Pringle repeated and with more conviction than he felt. "Won't be long now." Blast the NHS cutbacks, curse privatization. When in the name of humanity would somebody come!

Eternity lasted ten more minutes. The ambulance arrived and one of the men tried to help him to his feet so that the stretcher could be got into place. Shock swept over Mr Pringle in cold, sweaty waves. He continued to sit, legs outstretched, feeling wretchedly sick. A police driver appeared, exchanged brief muttered words with the ambulancemen, and crouched down beside him.

"You all right, sir?"

"He . . . he . . ." Mr Pringle swallowed.

"We'll see to him. You sit in my car till I get this lot sorted out, OK?"

A hand pulled him upright. Steadying himself against the policeman's shoulder, Mr Pringle saw that they'd pulled the blanket over the victim's head.

"Do be careful, he won't be able to breathe properly!"

"That's OK. You go and sit in the car," the young PC said quietly, and Mr Pringle realized that in those few moments, without him even noticing, the man had died.

He sat deep in misery with the radio crackling loudly. They'd thrust his belongings into the car. Among them Mr Pringle saw that he'd been given the blood-stained plastic carrier bag by mistake. He raised a feeble hand to attract their attention, but the ambulance was already pulling away. No matter, he'd let the policeman deal with it. Far more important, he realized, was his folded copy of the *Guardian*. There in the corner was the scribble: Fawn coloured Ford. Registration M, possibly MMB.

Of course, he remembered now. He'd been reminded of Mrs Bignell when he'd first noticed the car. Her second name was Muriel.

Studio A. Set and light

Some of the sets weren't properly lit and shadows added another dimension to the gloom. It wasn't cold, but one or two shivered as they moved about, and stage and prop hands spoke unnecessarily loudly to one another.

Beside her cage, clipboard in hand, Alix Baxter counted the number of surgical instruments very carefully. The unnaturally tense atmosphere made concentration difficult.

On the far side of the studio, sheets of plastic shrouded the ICU set. An outline in yellow tape on the floor indicated the boundary over which none must stray. Technicians quickened their pace at first, averting their eyes, but when nervousness began to fade they grew jaunty, knowing they'd avoided the Great Reaper this time and could afford to be a little more bold.

Alix ran her eye over the contents of her cage once more. It was pelmanism; halfway through a series she scarcely needed a second glance to know if all the props were there. The police had been insistent however, so she repeated the exercise, dutifully ticking them off against the list on her clipboard. When one of the prop hands came up behind her and spoke suddenly, she jumped.

"Christ! I didn't hear you."

"Sorry, I didn't mean to startle. Look what I found." The embossed silver picture frame lay in the palm of his hand.

"I never expected to see that again."

"It was behind a radiator near the upstairs dressing rooms. Fell out of someone's pocket and rolled underneath, I reckon." Alix turned it over. The backing was still in place, held by two of the four clips.

"No photograph."

"That must've fallen out. Bit of a laugh if whoever nicked it ended up with that instead."

"Be a love and find me a replacement, Jim. Not too modern, the woman's supposed to be Dr Watkins's mother. It belongs on the small table in his bedsit." She handed the frame back and Jim disappeared. Would the police be interested? She scribbled a note to remind herself.

Line-up was finished and cameramen dragged their Vintens away across the floor. The PA dashed after them with additional camera cards then hurried up the metal stairway to the control gallery. Robert was marshalling the actors with Bernard's agitation bursting through his cans. "We're fifty pages behind and we've already lost five minutes —" Robert pressed the talk button to stem the panic.

"Yes, Bernard. We're all aware. The two-bed ward first everyone, shot ninety-four on three. Nurse Williams plus patient. Doctors Carstairs and Watkins standing by."

In Wardrobe the call-boy was hastily allocating roles to extras.

"Iris, were you in the corridor set yesterday?"

"No, lovey."

"Then you're a patient in this scene, with Jacinta. Give Iris a dressing gown, Rita." The extra registered melodramatic anxiety as she thrust both arms into the sleeves. "Will one be safe, one asks oneself?"

"Of course you will. You'll be in shot the whole time!" He hustled her across the studio and on to the set. "Nurse Williams walks you over to the bed and helps you get into it, OK?" Any anxiety was replaced by pragmatism.

"Does Nurse Williams speak to me?"

"Only a couple of words."

"That makes me a Walk-on Two, dear. Kindly make a note of it."

"Oh, shit!"

"Robert, what the hell's the delay now?"

"Nearly there, Bernard." The floor manager moved swiftly. "What's up?"

"Iris says it makes her a Number Two."

"Walk-on One or we ask someone else." It was Hobson's choice. The extra capitulated gracefully.

"If you say so, Robert. Good morning, Miss Charles." Nurse Williams, pale and tense, took her arm. Bernard's tinny instructions came thick and fast through the cans.

"All I want on three are the two bodies passing through shot then we cut wide on two for Carstairs's entrance. Hold him on a two-shot at the bed with Jacinta. Lose the patient altogether but I want to see an anonymous lump in the bed for the final wide shot on three. Any questions? Right. We'll block then go straight for a take." Unseen by those on the floor, Bernard raised his hand in the control box and commanded, "Cue them."

"One moment." It was the new Walk-on One.

"For Christ's sake, Robert!"

"All right, Bernard. Yes, Iris?"

"What is my motivation?"

"You're a patient."

"Ah, yes. But what is the disease? Or is it surgery? And am I suffering from the after effects of medication?"

"She'll be suffering from a broken neck if I have to come down —"

"Just a sec, Bernard. Iris, all we want you to do is walk across and let Nurse Williams help you into bed."

"Following surgery?"

"Yes, if you like. Ready? And, cue!"

Wincing under the burden of her enfeebled body, the patient dragged herself the last few painful steps . . .

"CUT IT! Robert!"

"Iris, let's suppose you're about to be discharged. You're going back to bed for a little rest but you're not really ill any more. Can you manage that for me?" Iris smiled bravely. If she managed to delay the climb into bed, someone at Frinton might see and remember . . .

"Yes, Robert, I'm ready."

"First positions — and, cue."

On screen, a yard or so of woolly dressing gown went through frame and was gone.

60

As they were about to begin the second scene there was another hiatus.

"What now?" yelled the director dementedly.

"Sorry, Bernard. Break through on sound. Police siren or ambulance going past outside, I think."

"Listen, I have another forty-eight pages —"

"OK, OK —"

"We'll put it right at the dub. Roll tape and start the clock."

Piccadilly. Theatrical agent's office

Stone stairs led up to an old-fashioned heavy wooden door with glass panels. Inside all was modern and high-tech with minimal chairs designed to discourage prolonged visits. The office was an odd shape too, being contrived from a larger room, but it was peaceful thanks to efficient double-glazing. Beyond the spikey Italian desk lamp, Sylvia Mackenzie could see through the window the Café Royal and Aquascutum's spring display.

The agent stood with his back to the light, gazing out abstractedly. DPW Mackenzie had had no preconceived notion about theatrical offices, but she hadn't been expecting an elderly brown dog. It waddled across to have its ears tickled then flopped on to the geometric rug, duty done. Its master was a small, lithe man, tanned, bald and resigned.

"I shall miss Margarite. No more tantrums. She'd been with me for years, off and on. Kept coming back when she'd exhausted someone else's patience. I suppose United Allied put you on to me? She'd only been with them nine months. I've had her latest boyfriend Jason on the phone of course, telling me how it happened."

"If he knows, he'd better tell us!" DPW Mackenzie was annoyed.

"I should have said, Jason told me how the discovery was made," he corrected. "About the floor manager lifting the bedclothes, etc. What he told the *Sun*. He sounded far more terrified by threats from one of your officers than he did about the identity of the killer. So . . . someone else finally stuck the knife in. Rough justice, maybe? Can't say I'm surprised."

61

"So everyone keeps saying. Have you any idea who might have done it?" The agent shook his head.

"The list of possibilities is endless, but as to who finally took the decision yesterday . . . Margarite was a wonderful actress but she could be one hell of a bitch, couldn't she Morris?" The dog twitched an ear.

"Can you give me any personal background? We know about the marriage to Alfred Barker. What about recent attachments?" The man leaned back against elegant distressed pink leather.

"They've got younger and younger. She used to go for actors but lately she had to make do with models. I doubt whether there was anything sexual, but Margarite always needed a handsome face beside her. When Alfred gave her the push — that came as a terrific shock to her ego, by the way."

"Didn't she divorce him?"

"She did because Alfred was old-fashioned. He provided the evidence on condition the divorce went ahead. He continued to give her parts, mind you. Never held a grudge, especially after he'd married Kitty — very comfortable little body she is, the exact opposite. Anyway, Margarite was still a wonderful actress. The trouble was she fell out of favour when styles changed. Angry young playwrights in the sixties wanted leading ladies who could wear cardigans — not Margarite Pelouse. That's when she disappeared to the States and married another actor, Willie Henderson."

"Another?"

"Her first husband was, briefly, but he disappeared when profiles went out of fashion. Yes, popularity is a very transient thing, Miss. When I was young you had to look noble. Now, you don't even comb your hair and you can leave off shaving. It helps if you have talent of course."

"Apart from Jason Cornish, did Miss Pelouse have other friends?"

The agent shrugged. "Most people got bored with the cruel jokes. Willie kept in touch but then Margarite played a foul trick on his wife. It took a lot to upset Willie, I don't know whether his affection survived that. I can give you his address if you like?"

"Please." The small man moved neatly like an ex-dancer. He went over to the matt-black filing cabinet and found a card. "Here . . ."

The policewoman copied the details and asked casually, "I suppose actresses use their agents as confidants?"

"Some do. Depends if they're married or not. If they are, the husbands bear the brunt. Some come here to have a good cry when things go wrong . . . Morris is a godsend on those occasions. He can put up with any amount of salt water and cuddling. Margarite never moped, to be fair. She'd come to boast, or to show off the latest catch. It was the same pattern every time. It would be all ecstasy then the bitchiness would begin. There'd be one practical joke too many and she'd ring me up — usually the middle of the night — to complain that the current boy had walked out on her.

"When Jason told me no one had heard Margarite cry out yesterday, I wasn't surprised. She was getting bored with him and if another man walked on to that set it would never occur to her to be frightened; she'd be sizing him up as a possible replacement. The one thing she couldn't stand was being alone. In a way, I think it was partly a fear of dying. To have a virile young male in attendance made her feel both desirable and immortal."

DPW Mackenzie noted down in shorthand: "Agent convinced killer was male," and uncrossed her elegant legs.

"With her reputation it's a wonder any man would risk being enticed."

"Oh, but she could be charming, don't forget that." The agent held his hands wide, "You must remember Margarite wasn't English. She had that lavish European manner most of us shrink from, but with her it worked. If she wanted to, she could make you feel ten feet tall, the most desirable chap in the world." He spoke directly to the dog and his tanned face suddenly creased. "We've been in favour, haven't we Morris? Once. A long time ago."

DPW Mackenzie realized she must wait. She kept her voice impersonal when she eventually asked, "Was there anyone Miss Pelouse was friendly with in the cast of *Doctors and Nurses*?" He took the list and went where the light was better, speaking over his shoulder.

"Ian Walsh, of course. You know about him."

"We don't know any theatrical gossip." The agent was surprised.

"I suppose you wouldn't, not being in the profession. He and Jacinta Charles were close when they were drama students. A lot of young actors make that mistake. Cast 'em as Romeo and they imagine they're in love with Juliet . . ." He walked over to his filing cabinet again.

"The one bit of gossip we have been told is Jacinta Charles may have had some connection."

"There was more to it than that. Jacinta talked to a reporter on *The Stage* and claimed she was distantly related through her mother, to Margarite. I asked, naturally, but Margarite swore there wasn't a word of truth in it. I kept well out of it after that. Ah, this is what I was looking for . . ." It was a black and white photograph of a student production. Jacinta Charles in breeches stared up eagerly at Ian Walsh wearing a heavy furred gown.

"*Twelfth Night*. I tried to sign Jacinta up when I saw her in that. A good thing I didn't succeed. Especially when Margarite took her revenge. Wouldn't have wanted both ladies on my books after that happened." He sighed and stared at Sylvia Mackenzie. "One of her bloodiest tricks. Margarite made it her business to get to know Ian Walsh after that article appeared. She wanted to hit Jacinta where it would hurt most."

"And she succeeded?"

"Oh, yes. Margarite arranged it so that Walsh played opposite her in a revival of *The Way of the World*. It was a limited run, out of town, ideal for her purpose. By the end of it, Walsh was besotted and Jacinta Charles had lost him."

He saw the young policewoman's expression and shook his head. "I know what you're thinking, Miss. What a spineless chap, eh? How could a youngster fall for an old woman? But you see when she wanted to, Margarite could be magic."

Programme controller's office
The police car driver had helped him up the steps and left him in

Reception. Now Mr Pringle was on Ashley's sofa, his head between his knees, at the tender mercy of the feminist from Camden Passage. Angela bounced indignantly out of Ashley's private washroom carrying a bowl.

"Are you likely to need this again?" Mr Pringle dearly wanted to say "yes" but was too frightened.

"I think I'll be all right."

"Thank God for that."

"I'm sorry to be such a nuisance." He caught sight of his bloody sleeve and his stomach heaved. Angela thrust the bowl under his nose.

"Men!" There was all the contempt in the world in her voice. The outer door opened and Ashley walked in. She turned to greet him.

"Your friend here has done nothing but spew for the last half-hour."

"G B H? Why, whatever's happened?"

"Someone was run over and he happened to be passing, that's all —"

"That must have been why there were diversions in Broadwick Street —"

"He stayed with the bloke till he died and then came in here to throw up. The point is, I do not come here to clean up sick —"

"Do me a favour, doll, I haven't had a coffee yet —"

"Nor to act as a minion."

"A what?"

Angela deposited the bowl with a crash, "Let me know when you want your correspondence dealt with."

The door banged and Ashley winced. "Why do they invent women like that? I mean — why? My friends are much prettier and they have nicer manners. How that one ever got herself pregnant, I do not know. Maybe she put her eggs in one of those little glass dishes where the sperm can't escape —"

"Aah . . . !"

"Can you make it?" Ashley broke off from his reverie to point urgently to the washroom door, "Through there."

"I don't think I'm going to be ill, thanks."

"It must've been a nasty shock."

"It was dreadful — he was killed, you see." Ashley clicked his tongue.

"Terrible." But he was turning on the television and selecting Studio A channel, "Don't think me callous, harte, but Bernard was fifty pages behind when he began this morning and if they've arrested Jacinta as well . . ."

On screen there was a close-up of Nurse Williams which immediately made Ashley happy. "Oh, good, there she is. Sergeant Cork obviously hasn't been told she killed Margarite. With a bit of luck we might get all her scenes recorded before someone spills the beans."

"The accident victim appeared to be on his way here." Ashley swivelled round.

"He wasn't one of the cast, was he? Richard'll go spare if he's got to write another one out."

"I'm not sure who he was. I don't normally watch *Doctors and Nurses*."

"Let's hope it was one of the crew," Ashley was cheerfully indifferent. "We can always get hold of a freelance cameraman. Actors are different. We need continuity in a cast — until *we* decide they have to go, of course." He grew pensive. "I hope you're wrong about that chap, though. If he *was* coming here, well . . . These things usually go in threes."

There was a knock and a burly man put his head round the door. "Photograph wanted, name of Pringle?"

"That's right, come on in." The man saw the slumped, whey-faced figure and blinked.

"Blimey, what part's he come for, Yorick?"

"It's only a staff pass!"

"Oh, well then." The burly man walked over and asked persuasively, "Ready to have your picture taken, sir?" Mr Pringle struggled to his feet.

"Not really."

"Never mind. It won't hurt, like the dentist. Here . . ." he called as he snapped and clicked, "heard what happened to Bertie? He got himself knocked over."

"Bertie Bowman?"

"That's right. Stupid old bugger, he was probably drunk. They

66

took him off in an ambulance but I reckon he'd had it. That's it, Mr Pringle. Your pass should be ready later on today."

"Thank you." Mr Pringle didn't bother to ask for a copy. When the photographer had gone he enquired, "Was Mr Bowman a member of the cast?"

"He was an extra," Ashley replied. "We used him regularly, for sentimental reasons." This was a new aspect of television: caring for the well-being of employees? Mr Pringle felt compelled to ask whether he'd heard aright.

"Some extras are former actors who've fallen on hard times. We use them whenever we can." But Ashley dismissed all thought of a dead extra who, like a crew-member, could easily be replaced. "'Ere, you know what you said about mourning, harte. I saw the most divine cashmere coat in Jasper Conran's; it had a black fleck in the lining."

Mr Pringle was beginning to wish he'd never mentioned the possibility. "Last night I reached the bottom of the pile of demands, Fallowfield. I think it would be wise if we didn't rely on the Revenue's indulgence more than we have to, don't you?"

ITCHY SPOTS

The Rose & Crown. Tuesday lunchtime
Rita Phelps hadn't the bulk to force her way through the
lunchtime drinkers so used her own method; jabbing in the
general area of the kidneys and when the owner turned to
glare, giving a smile that revealed her ghastly teeth. As usual,
a passage opened up before her.

"Are you on your lonesome?"

When Ian Walsh saw who it was he kept his face blank and
his voice neutral. "Looks like it."

The wardrobe mistress squeezed in and sat down. Reluctantly, he rose.

"I'll have a Mirage and tonic, thanks."

"What on earth's that?"

"They know. I've had one here before. With ice." Walsh
forced his way through to the bar and returned with a single
glass containing apricot-coloured fluid.

"You not having another?"

"No."

"Very sensible. You want to keep your wits about you while
the Fuzz are still poking their noses in." The actor glanced at
her briefly then looked away. Rita crept a little nearer her
objective. "That's why I wanted a private word." She waited
again, confident he would break first.

"What about?"

She smirked. "About your visit to Margarite in her tent
yesterday morning. When Justin excused himself for a bit of
peace and quiet and you nipped inside. You thought no one
saw, but I did." She had his full attention now. Ian Walsh
made himself sound calm.

"Margarite and I were old friends."

"I'll say you were." The inference was unmistakable.

"You eavesdropped," he said flatly.

"You can't help overhearing when people forget to lower their voices." Despite his good intention, Walsh flared up.

"You listened deliberately because you can't resist poking *your* nose in, can you, Rita?"

"No need to be unpleasant."

"So what's all this about?"

"I thought you wouldn't want it generally known, what you were discussing with Madame Pelouse."

"Bloody hell!" He moved so violently, his empty glass rolled on to the floor. Rita's drink slopped into her lap.

"Watch it!"

"If that's your game, forget it!" Ian Walsh didn't lower his voice this time either. One or two turned to stare, recognized him and began nudging one another. "You thought you'd try a bit of blackmail — going to threaten me with the police, were you Rita? You're too late. I've already decided to tell them everything, including the fact that you once threatened to murder Margarite yourself."

"It's a lie!"

"Not according to dear old Henry, it isn't."

"The old —!"

"I'm sure you can think of a satisfactory explanation — when the police ask for one." Ian Walsh strode out leaving Rita the sole object of the fascinated lunchtime crowd.

Police Station. Office adjacent to incident room
Frank Newton was still feeling bilious, enough to miss out on lunch. It was an ideal time to collect his thoughts and sift through the morning's completed Actions. He responded to the second knock.

"Yes?"

"Excuse me, sir. A Miss Jacinta Charles is outside asking to speak to someone."

"Are either of the DPWs about?"

"Doreen isn't back yet. Sylvia's at lunch."

69

"Page the canteen for her and ask Miss Charles to wait. I'll ring when we're ready."

He'd been brooding since he returned from the autopsy. He had the interim medical report and considered what he'd seen at the mortuary; four stab wounds, three of which could have been fatal. An indication, according to Pavis, of increasing panic on the part of the killer. It was also a virtual certainty that whoever it was had been left-handed. How theatrical, Newton sniffed, but then, how appropriate. The inquest was scheduled for three p.m. that afternoon.

In the incident room one of the operators was adding another statistic to the computer file: the hit and run in Lexington Street. Bowman had been declared dead on arrival at hospital. Newton had asked to be informed of any findings. There might be a connection; he kept an open mind at this stage.

"Thank you for coming, Miss Charles."

"I guessed it was only a matter of time before you sent for me."

"Please smoke if you wish." Jacinta was tempted but didn't; she needed to keep something in reserve. Goodness knows how long this would take or whether she'd be allowed cigarettes afterwards. She examined the room quickly; one table, three chairs, one ashtray, nothing else apart from a ghastly smell of disinfectant. She was so tense she barely registered DPW Mackenzie alongside the inspector.

"Could we have a window open?"

"I'd rather we didn't," Newton apologized. "The din can be off-putting." Jacinta gave a tight smile.

"Of course. Stupid of me, I wasn't thinking." Oh, but you were, thought Newton, you're so keyed up you might snap.

"If we could go through one or two points Miss Charles, then we might have a cup of tea."

"I want to explain my personal connection with Margarite Pelouse."

"I've been told of the article in *The Stage*, but I haven't seen it yet."

"The facts it contained were correct. Briefly, my mother was a niece of Margarite Pelouse's first husband, my grandmother being his baby sister. Great-Uncle Gilbert was working abroad when he met and married Margarite, or Erika as she then was. Back in England the marriage didn't last and they divorced. I only discovered my great-uncle's existence after my mother died. She and I weren't close because she disapproved enormously of my choice of a career. He was considered another black sheep of the family too, I've no idea why; no one ever spoke of him. I was delighted when I discovered not only that I had another uncle but from a reference in a letter, that his ex-wife subsequently became Margarite Pelouse."

"I understand Miss Pelouse didn't respond to the article or your claim?" Frank Newton noted the twitchy anger opposite. "Was it jealousy?" he asked quietly. "Did Miss Pelouse see in you an attractive young actress who might steal her limelight?"

"Not a chance," Jacinta burst out. "She was an established star, but she behaved like a bitch. She certainly did respond: she behaved as though I'd threatened her. First she said she'd prosecute then she filched my boyfriend." Without realizing, Jacinta had lit a cigarette. "I don't know whether Ian and I would have lasted," she admitted, "but we were blissfully happy until he went on that tour."

"Why raise the matter so publicly? Why not a note explaining you'd discovered the family connection?" Jacinta reddened.

"I kidded myself that it was a marvellous opportunity to declare how proud I was to be related. Afterwards, when it all went sour, I realized I'd been a fool. Of course I'd hoped Margarite would pull strings when she discovered she had a relative. In our business, we go down on our knees for a bit of nepotism."

"Yes, I believe it can be tough. Perhaps we should begin in the usual way by asking for your full name, address and age, Miss Charles —"

"I spoke to Margarite yesterday," Jacinta interrupted abruptly.

"Oh, yes?" He looked up from his pad. "When was this?"

"When she was in the ICU set." Frank Newton remained impassive.

"Did anyone see you speak to her?"

71

"I don't think so. I used the door of the set and the screens hid us from the studio. I wanted a quiet tête à tête. I'd just had a row with — one of the cameramen. About the article, naturally. Everyone remembers it. Ever since Margarite was brought in as a replacement, they were waiting for me to tackle her. Simon accused me of being gutless and goaded me by suggesting none of it was true. Margarite hadn't moved from the rehearsal room without Jason Cornish beside her, so the first opportunity was yesterday, while the studio was busy with the corridor scene."

"And she spoke to you?"

"Oh, yes." Jacinta made an effort at a joke, "She was definitely alive when I left the set."

"What exactly did you say to her?"

"I asked why she'd been so hostile. Why, after all these years, couldn't she acknowledge the connection with my great-uncle?"

"And what was her reply?"

"She ignored my question. She told me to get out and her last words were that if I dared approach her again, she'd see to it my contract at Rainbow Television was terminated. I was so upset I took myself off to the Ladies to recover instead of waiting to do the scene."

"Had Miss Pelouse the power to have you fired?" Jacinta looked bleak.

"I expect so," she said dully. "Margarite's managed to destroy plenty of other people and no one's irreplaceable in a soap. It's just an illusion we all cherish."

"One important question, Miss Charles. Have you any idea why anyone should kill Miss Pelouse?" Her face was full of the same hopelessness.

"Someone with a better motive than mine, you mean? I wish I had."

It was half an hour later, when DPW Mackenzie was labor-iously typing out the final words of the statement that DS Mullin arrived in the incident room. The business of obtaining everyone's details was nearly complete and he had important news. Frank Newton took him to a quiet corner.

"Walsh has admitted speaking to the victim yesterday, sir. He said they had a row."

Margarite Pelouse's final moments certainly hadn't lacked drama, Newton reflected.

"When was this?"

"While she was in the quick-change tent. Jason Cornish had nipped off for a pee so Walsh took the opportunity and slipped inside."

"Did he say why?"

"He was a bit cagey. We didn't have much time because he was about to start acting again. He's promised to make a full statement when he's finished this evening. It'll be after eight o'clock unfortunately, as he's in practically every scene."

"Hard luck," said Newton.

"I thought you might want to be there?"

"No point. Phone me if he says anything important, otherwise I'll read it in the morning. Anyone else admit to bending the victim's ear? Or better still, stabbing her?"

"No. Several wanted to talk about the chap who was run over. He used to be in films, apparently." It wasn't Frank Newton's problem.

"We've got enough on our plate. I think I'd like a chat with Henry Titmouse."

"They break in about fifteen minutes. I've got a copy of their recording schedule so we know where to lay our hands on any one we need."

"Good. Just time for a quick chat with Titmouse and a sandwich before the inquest."

"Any joy with Miss Charles?"

"She's made a statement. It sounds plausible but then again, she is a thespian." The man from Leicester was unaware of Jean Newton's former profession.

"I know. Can't trust a thing any of those poofters and tarts tell you."

Programme controller's office
Ashley had invited him to lunch but Mr Pringle preferred to

73

remain where he was, peace and quiet were what he needed. He'd cleaned the worst of the blood off himself and the carrier bag, and obtained Angela's permission to make himself a cup of tea. He now felt well enough to tackle the pile of staff expenses Ashley had asked him to check but Jo, the make-up supervisor, intervened.

"Are you busy?"

"No, no, do come in. I'm afraid Fallowfield won't be back until two p.m."

"It's you I wanted to see, actually." She waved a familiar looking envelope. "Is it true you understand income tax?"

At Bath & Wells Television, Mr Pringle had been dazzled by the glamour of the make-up department. This supervisor behind earnest spectacles was too comfortable to thrill but her admiration warmed the cockles of his heart.

"Aren't you wonderful! You make it all sound so easy! Wait till I tell my girls, they'll be queuing to have theirs filled in. Did you say there was a query about my expenses?"

Hers was a simple matter and Jo was a docile creature when it came to pointing out an error. Mr Pringle was relieved. He'd already had an acerbic phone conversation with one of the electricians who refused to be persuaded that journeying from home to work wasn't an allowable claim.

"What a shame you witnessed Bertie's accident this morning." They'd settled on a more modest figure for Jo and her concern was now for him. "Bertie was a dear — a bit inclined to ramble on the way a lot of them do — but a gentleman. Old-fashioned. If he had a rose in his buttonhole, he'd always give it to one of my girls at the end of the day. We shall miss him."

Mr Pringle wondered aloud if anyone had expressed sadness at Margarite Pelouse's passing. Jo pursed her lips.

"I know she could be — well, awkward. But she was very professional. She started being difficult in Make-up first thing yesterday morning so I had a little word. She was as good as gold after that."

"Why was that, do you know?" he asked out of curiosity.

"I'm not sure. She was a bundle of nerves. We can always tell, you can feel tension under the skin. I had more coffee sent down. She began to unwind after that."

"How strange, with all her experience —"

"It wasn't stage fright," Jo shook her head vigorously. "That's quite different. I think Margarite was — anxious." Mr Pringle looked grave.

"You must tell the police; it could be important."

"Two of them in two days! It's really frightening." Jo shuddered. He tried to reassure her.

"The police seemed confident the hit and run driver will soon be found."

"And you'll be able to identify him."

"Oh, I doubt it."

"You know what they're saying? It could have been the same man who sneaked in here yesterday and killed Margarite."

"Surely that's extremely unlikely? What possible connection could there be?"

"Most of us don't believe Jacy could have done it."

"Oh, I see. Well, I fear it must have been someone Miss Pelouse knew otherwise she would have raised the alarm. Nor can I guarantee to identify the driver. I didn't see his face, simply the back of his head and part of the number plate."

Jo's faith in him was unswerving. "I read a book once. It said however well you disguise your face, it's impossible to alter your back view. It's true. I should know."

"I wish that I could . . ." Terror froze his tongue and began seeping into the cracks, making his muscles sag. Jo saw his expression change and tried to guess at the cause.

"You won't be too scared to pick him out, will you?"

He didn't reply because he'd realized that although he couldn't recognize the driver, he'd been hovering on the kerb worrying about traffic wardens quite long enough for the man to get a good look at him.

"What's the matter?" Jo asked. Mr Pringle licked dry lips.

"Fallowfield's remark . . . that these things go in threes."

Female extras' dressing room

The four female non-speakers unwrapped their packets of food coyly. Financial strictures were rarely admitted even if they were tight. Social etiquette however, was rigidly observed.

"I never travel without my own plate and glass even when it's location caterers. 'You can throw that melamine away,' I tell them. 'I am accustomed to eating off china.' Some of them can be so rude. One man hinted it's because of Aids."

"That's a pretty pattern, is it Spode?" It wasn't, therefore the owner felt smug and changed the subject.

"Bertie had his own little cup, d'you remember? Gold coloured. It was part of his hip flask. He used to say that came from Aspreys."

"No doubt it did. If only he hadn't been so upset by yesterday's events, I'm sure he wouldn't have been so careless this morning." The doyenne, Iris, gave her opinion from within the only comfortable chair. She had frayed damask rather than a paper towel over her knees. "I sincerely hope *The Stage* doesn't omit to mention his early career."

"D'you think he'll get an obituary?" The extra who'd asked became awkward under Iris's glare. "I mean, bit-part players don't usually qualify."

"He used to be an artiste," Iris insisted fiercely, anxious for her own posterity.

"He was past it." The fourth girl chewed stolidly. The glamour of working in television had begun to tarnish and she was contemplating a switch to word-processing, to her mother's infinite relief. "He forgot what he was doing half the time. Yesterday I had to push him on in the first scene, he wasn't watching for his cue." Iris sprang to the defence of a colleague.

"Mr Bowman was a trooper, he never let anyone down! I for one, will honour him." She groped in her bag, pulled out a glass, a miniature of gin, a half empty bottle of tonic and a seedy looking lemon which she proceeded to slice defiantly.

"Was he at Frinton then?" the fourth girl demanded. "Is that where you met?" Iris didn't even deign to look up.

"If you must know, Mr Bowman joined us for a week during a disastrous summer season at Colwyn Bay," she answered coldly. "He took over as juve lead in *For Goodness' Sake* when someone was ill. I remember his as the only inspiration among some wretchedly amateur performances." She raised her glass, "To an artiste," she announced sententiously. In the embarrassed

76

silence the fourth girl spoke, as if unaware of her social gaff.

"Have you heard there's someone at the studios who can sort out your income tax? If you want an appointment, you ring Angela in Ashley Fallowfield's office. He's quite cheap, not like an accountant."

Studio A. Wardrobe room
Henry Titmouse was busy even though it was the lunchbreak. He was flustered, not simply because Newton was questioning him, but because Rita hovered like a malevolent crow. "I daren't stop, sir," he begged. "We're behindhand today. The director keeps changing the running order so we don't know where we are. I shall get into more trouble if the continuity isn't right."

"Don't worry," Newton calmed him, "it'll keep till later, it's not that important." The elderly, childlike face was pathetically grateful, but Newton had no intention of asking for information in front of Rita Phelps. He nodded to her cursorily.

"They want to know about that gown, that's what it is," she prompted, fuelling Henry's agitation. "They don't think you've told them all you know. Withholding evidence, that's what it's called."

"But I have!" Acutely distressed, Henry pleaded with Newton, "I told the police lady everything I could remember yesterday."

"It's all right," Newton itched to strangle Rita. "Some other time." He left the room to the sound of Henry's plaintive: "I told the lady there wasn't a drop of blood on it when I put it in Ian's dressing room, Rita . . ."

In the passage, Newton hesitated. "We've still got a few minutes . . . the stage-manager will be at lunch — don't let me forget I haven't spoken to her yet. Is Jason Cornish about?"

"I don't think so. He wasn't part of the production."

"Of course. I think you're right. We should pull him in again — I'm damn sure he didn't tell us all he knew, either. When Pelouse's bank manager can be persuaded to tell us what the financial arrangements —" A peremptory cry of "I say!" made them turn. The PA was hurrying towards them, laden with scripts, clipboard and her stop-watch.

"Sorry to interrupt but it is vitally important." Newton was gracious.

"Certainly, Miss —"

"Pat Fagan," prompted Mullin.

"Miss Fagan."

"You haven't arrested Jacy yet, have you? We've just spot-checked the tape and there's drop-out all over her scenes!"

"We told Miss Charles she was free to go."

"Oh, thank God for that! The tape's completely unusable. We'll have to do those scenes again and it means hours of overtime. Bernard's hysterical. He's had three nose-bleeds and he's started talking to the rubber plant."

"Artistic temperament getting the better of him?" suggested Mullin.

"What a quaint idea. Bernard wouldn't know what that was. No, he's going through the male menopause. It's hell on earth getting him to make decisions at the moment and his wife doesn't help. She's constantly on the phone because the Aga's on the blink. But the thing I really must know is, are you about to arrest anyone else?"

Newton stared at the bossily efficient face, totally oblivious to anything apart from the immediate needs of one television soap. The nerve beneath his temple began to twitch.

"It's difficult to say at the moment Miss Fagan — " he began.

"Because if you are," Pat interrupted impatiently, "you must let *me* know beforehand." She saw that understanding was slow. "So that Bernard and I can rejig the schedule, you see. It's surely not too much to ask? After all, we're doing absolutely everything we can to co-operate." Exasperated though he was, Newton realized this incredible nanny-figure was utterly sincere. He struggled to sound polite.

"I'll bear your request in mind."

"Oh, good! As soon as you tell me who you want to arrest, we'll change the running order," Pat assured him, "OK? Now you must excuse me, I am rather busy." She gave a professional smile, but her mind was already grappling with the next problem. Newton watched her hurry away.

"Let her know beforehand!" he muttered.

"I suppose they think it's important," offered Mullin. "All they ever do is make telly programmes."

The inquest into Margarite Pelouse's death opened and closed within minutes and occupied one and a half column inches on page two of the *Evening Standard*. Already her star was beginning to fade. Newton avoided the lone photographer outside the Coroner's Court, booked a table at his local Greek restaurant and remembered to phone the babysitter. He couldn't really afford an evening out this week, but it might mend a bridge or two with Jean. She'd been confined at home too long, he acknowledged to himself. And a leisurely early meal might soothe his own indigestion.

Surgery on outskirts of Hendon

It was a busy, shabby clinic with only one GP. He did his best but didn't have time to waste during evening surgery. He had this patient's notes in front of him and was trying vainly to remember something about the man. The most recent entry dated back to 1984.

"And what seems to be the trouble?"

"I can't sleep." The man spoke so quietly the doctor had to strain to hear.

"That's a symptom not a disease, Mr Goodman. How long since you had a check-up?"

"*Hill*," said the man half-apologetically. The doctor glanced again at the card.

"Goodhill, sorry. I must do something about these spectacles!" It was a joke and it irritated him that so few patients found it amusing. "So, how long since I saw you last?"

"I don't think we've ever met . . . it's over four years since I last came. After my daughter's — accident." The doctor scanned the notes.

79

"Which was before my time," he said absently. The man agreed but didn't say so. "I see you had sleeping pills then." Disapproval was obvious. "I want you to make an appointment for a full clinical examination. See the receptionist before you go, if you would. Meanwhile we'll just check one or two things while you're here — jacket off please and roll up your sleeve. Any pressures at work?"

"Just a few pills, to help me sleep," the man implored. "If I could have one good night it might break the pattern." In the days after Anne was killed drugged oblivion was all that he craved. Four years later, surely they couldn't deny him a brief taste of it again?

The doctor tried to be tolerant. "Let's see if we can't improve your general health first, Mr Goodhill. Make a new man of you, eh?"

Rainbow Television. Reception

It was always a quiet time, five minutes before the end of recording at eight p.m. Behind Studio A's sound-proof doors, Bernard was approaching his first heart attack, but here the security man brooded peacefully over Arsenal. DS Mullin waited impatiently on the banquette for Walsh to appear.

Mullin had decided to use his initiative. The atmosphere of the incident room wasn't, in his opinion, conducive to relaxed conversation. Once the staff had gone home and the computers were switched off, it was quiet enough but witnesses often found the silence oppressive. A noisy pub might, in theory, produce better results.

Ian Walsh was among the first to emerge. When he saw Mullin he said stiffly, "I hadn't forgotten. I was coming straight over to the police station."

"I wondered if you might prefer a bite to eat while we talked, Mr Walsh. Or a pint. I know I'm ready for one. Didn't manage any lunch today."

"I was threatened with blackmail," Ian Walsh said wryly. "It ruined my appetite." Mullin waited until he'd handed in his key and they'd emerged on to wet Soho pavements.

"Who was it did that?"

"Rita Phelps. How about a pizza? I'm always starving after a heavy day."

Mullin walked solidly along beside him thinking "heavy day"? The poofter didn't know what he was talking about. Italian food wasn't his idea of a meal either, being a pie and pint man.

The floor was tiled, there were red tablecloths, candles in Chianti bottles and the waiters appeared genuinely interested in their customers' welfare. Ian Walsh ordered, handed back the menu and relaxed for the first time that day. Mullin wondered if the steak would be covered in garlic and enquired gloomily whether they did draught beer.

When the wine had been poured, Walsh reverted to his earlier topic. "Our revered wardrobe mistress . . . it's a wonder no one's bumped her off before now."

"Oh, yes?" Mullin tasted the vinegary brew scouring parts that beer never interfered with.

"She eavesdropped on my — my row — with Margarite and thought she could put the squeeze on."

"Did she now."

"Which is why I want to give a full account of every single word that was said," Walsh said cheerfully. "Although it doesn't include a confession to murder, I'm afraid." Naturally, thought Mullin.

"What was the row about, sir?"

"Margarite and I once had a sort of affair."

Good God, thought Mullin, she was old enough to be his gran!

"Nothing sexual. She was too old for that." For some reason, this disgusted Mullin even more. "I was besotted with her," Ian Walsh admitted. "No doubt you find that odd."

"Not at all, sir, no." For an amateur Mullin was giving an excellent performance.

"We were on tour, playing opposite one another. The attraction simply continued after the curtain fell. Margarite intended that it should. The trouble was, I was then living with Jacinta Charles."

"Ah."

"And I wrote letters to Margarite after the tour was over . . . which she kept." Mullin began to see a glimmer of light.

"Were you hoping now that you and Miss Charles would eventually . . . ?"

"Resume our former relationship? Something like that. I'd certainly come to my senses over Margarite. I realized as soon as I saw her again that she'd done it deliberately, simply to separate Jacy and I. Jacy's friendly with one of the cameramen but without sounding vain, I think that was on the rebound. I don't think she's really keen — and he is married."

"Ah," said Mullin again. "These letters, Mr Walsh." Letters were facts, ink and paper evidence; not the sticky slippery morass of emotional upset.

"Margarite threatened to send them to Jacinta."

"And you wanted to stop that happening. Did you ask for them back?"

"I intended to. What I actually said was that she was a miserable old bitch who was living up to her reputation for destroying other people's happiness."

"Not exactly persuasive."

"She wouldn't part with them, it was futile." Walsh shook his head.

"I see." Mullin looked down at his spaghetti alla carbonara and remembered he didn't like cream sauce. He took a mouthful and washed the taste away with the wine. "What did you do when she refused, sir?" Walsh had done the right thing in ordering whitebait, he noticed.

"Nothing. It might sound feeble but I simply went in that tent to ask for them without Jason Cornish being present. I'd forgotten how rotten Margarite could be. She really enjoyed making me grovel — that's when it developed into a row — which Rita overheard."

"Were any threats made, sir?" Walsh pulled a face.

"Possibly."

"Oh, come Mr Walsh." The actor took a sip of wine. Mullin observed bitterly that the pansy was actually enjoying the muck. He repeated more sharply, "Was anything said?"

"I heard you. Yes, there was. Threats, in fact. But I'd no intention of carrying them out."

"Any — specific — threat?"

"I told Margarite if she tried to spoil it with Jacy, I'd kill her. But I didn't."

"Quite." Walsh pushed his whitebait aside. Mullin looked at it longingly then pulled himself together.

"I think we'll go to the station after we've finished here, Mr Walsh. It would be better if you made a full statement." The actor went pale but kept his voice even.

"You're not intending to charge me, I hope?"

"Not at present, sir, no. That will be up to Detective Inspector Newton." Unaccustomed wine made Mullin jovial. "After all, we know where to find you tomorrow, don't we? In the studio, scalpel in hand. Waiter, you can take this lot away."

"Concerning Rita Phelps." Ian Walsh fiddled with a fork. "Henry reckons he overheard her saying she'd kill Margarite. I realize it's second-hand tittle-tattle but I thought you ought to know."

"We'll look into it," Mullin promised, "tomorrow." Had anyone not threatened to kill the old biddy, he wondered.

On the way to the station, Mullin was conscious of his heavy pace compared to the lithe strides of the actor. The bloke wore his clothes better, too. Mullin always reckoned a sweater round the shoulders looked cissy, but on Walsh it didn't. They walked in silence for a while.

"This — dressing-up business — you've got to admit that's all acting is, really. What's it like spending your life pretending to be someone else? I must admit I find it difficult to understand why any grown-up should want to do it as a full-time job." It never occurred to Mullin that boorishness might be offensive. Why bother being tender with a murder suspect, after all?

"You don't watch television, Sergeant?"

"No. The wife switches it on, of course."

"Of course. But you don't watch because you're too busy. It's interesting how many people are."

"Oh, I put up with it. I may even have seen you. The wife knew who you were straight away. When I phoned home last night, she said . . ." But what Mrs Mullin had demanded was that her beloved should bring home an autograph and Mullin was buggered if he'd demean himself by asking for one. Ian Walsh gave a twisted smile.

"We are such stuff as dreams are made of, Sergeant."

"Come again?"

"Let's hope your wife isn't dreaming of one of us." I overstepped the mark that time, thought Ian Walsh.

You shouldn't have said that, thought Detective Sergeant Mullin.

Mr Pringle's kitchen

Mavis decided to visit, unexpectedly, and Mr Pringle was never more glad to see anyone. Shock had left him weak. Now, trying to rinse away blood from the sleeve of his coat, he felt horribly sick.

"What on earth — Oh, my Lord! You haven't been trying to slit your wrists!"

"Don't be silly!" He no longer felt sick, he was in a huff.

"No, of course you haven't," Mavis agreed. "You'd do it some other way — but how did you get in such a state?"

She listened in silence. She went to the fridge and shook her head over the contents, found tins in the larder instead and began opening them with abandon. "Don't argue. You look like death warmed up and I bet you haven't eaten all day?"

Mr Pringle admitted a small degree of neglect. Mavis noticed the carrier bag.

"Did you remember to get any bread?"

"That's not mine. It belonged to . . . to Mr Bowman. I meant to take it to the police station but I didn't feel well enough. I'll go there first thing tomorrow." Mavis inspected the contents without compunction.

"I don't suppose he had a loaf —"

"Mavis! We can't touch what's in there."

"Well, it won't be much use to him, dear. Anyway, there's not. It's just his bits and pieces —"

"Please." Mr Pringle was sensitive over the loss of a fellow human's dignity. Mavis put the carrier aside.

"Don't upset yourself, dear. Would you like me to stay tonight?"

84

She folded him in her generous arms and wrapped her warm body round his shivering flesh, but she couldn't banish the terrors of the night.

"It wasn't the fact that he died — it was the way it happened . . . in the street. No one ought to die like that."

"It was quick, you said."

"Not really. He saw the car before it hit him. I think he knew what was happening."

"But he didn't want anyone blamed. Perhaps he thought it was his own fault? If he didn't look where he was going —"

"He just stood there, rooted to the spot." Mavis sighed.

"They say rabbits act like that when they see a ferret. Even though they can run faster, fright paralyses them. Maybe it was like that with Mr Bowman." Mr Pringle wasn't convinced. "He sounds a nice old man, perhaps he didn't want to die blaming anyone," Mavis insisted. "It could have been an accident."

Mr Pringle didn't bother to argue, he was too tired. Besides, when he took the carrier to the police station there might be news. The vast machine had probably already pin-pointed the identity of the driver. So long as he wasn't called on to identify him . . . Mr Pringle fell into a troubled sleep.

Olympia restaurant

They weren't regular customers, they didn't visit often enough, but the proprietor's wife remembered Frank Newton preferred a quiet corner table. She watched sentimentally as he made sure his wife was comfortable and insisted they have two glasses of Ouzo "on the house". You never knew when it might be useful to have a friend among the police. She remembered the warrant card falling on to the table when this customer once fumbled for his credit card.

Newton waited until she'd waddled away before raising his glass. "To my lovely wife . . . may she always remember to come back." Jean pulled one of her monkey faces.

"Sorry about last night. I'm not terribly good with a mass of eight-year-olds."

He reached for her hand. "You're heroic. I'm sorry I had to let you down." They settled on their order before he asked, "Tell

85

me about a play called *The Way of the World*?" Immediately, Jean began to sparkle.

"Mmm, lovely Restoration piece. Comedy of manners, very stylish, by Congreve. Edith Evans was reputedly marvellous in it."

"So, I understand, was Margarite Pelouse."

"Of course! She revived it with Ian Walsh." Newton watched, half-jealous as his wife slipped away inside her memories. That wasn't why he'd brought them here tonight. Conscientiousness meant that he kept up the line of questioning.

"What surprises me is how a young man could be realistically cast opposite a much older woman," but Jean was ready with her answer.

"On stage, you wouldn't be aware, it's all to do with the illusion of theatre. Everyone has wigs and lots of make-up. A sort of enamelled look, whitened skin, black patches and plenty of rouge. And gorgeous costumes. You can disguise yourself at any age in those and the audience wouldn't notice because it's all part of the magic."

"I suppose so." It was faintly absurd to Frank Newton. "Is there a lot of lovey-dovey in the play?"

"Gawd!" It hurt that she didn't bother to hide her derision. "You're asking about one of the most witty, polished comedies ever written."

"What I meant was do they end up going to bed together?"

"It's far more titillating and sensual than simple bonking!" Jean was overexcited because she'd consumed most of the wine. "Millament and Mirabell practically eat one another in the most wonderful exchange of words. Every line is an innuendo." The mobile face was alight now. Newton could sense she was about to flick open an imaginary fan and reached across to catch her hand.

"Tell you what . . . Let's go to bed and you can show me how it goes."

It was about three a.m. that he jerked awake suddenly and cursed. "Oh, shit! How stupid can you be!" After that it was impossible to sleep. He lay there tossing restlessly until he could decently get up and make the tea.

6

UNWELCOME PROGNOSIS

Mr Pringle's study. Wednesday morning

Mr Pringle stood at the window, jingling the coins in his pockets. Mavis had let him sleep late because of her concern and he'd telephoned Ashley to say he wouldn't be in before lunch. He couldn't rid his memory of Fallowfield's remark that "things" usually went in threes. Superstition Mr Pringle despised, but events of the past two days plus a broken night had shaken his confidence. Every time he'd closed his eyes he dreamed of Bowman and the way his head had turned when he heard the car. It was an actor's profile surmounted by wavy, silvery hair; but it was the despair in the eyes that haunted Mr Pringle. He woke, sweating from his nightmare.

The next blow arrived in the post. One of the roofing gentlemen, the one he'd disliked least, had previously given what he called "a verbal". The written estimate arrived in a package commensurate with its newly found proportions and the postman had to ring the bell.

"They make nice big letter boxes nowadays, not difficult to fit."

"No." For Mr Pringle a hammer applied to a nail usually ended in a crisis.

He'd taken the package up to his study to open; he had a sense of foreboding when he felt the good quality envelope. The glossy appearance of the contents fooled him at first. He assumed the folder bound with a tasselled cord contained a brochure and lingered over the artwork before untying the bow.

Inside, exquisitely laid out, was a summary of the gentleman's further deliberations. Plus VAT. Immediately, Mr Pringle was in a panic. He realized he could not, under any circumstances, afford a new roof. There were words which necessitated a dictionary, but a fuller understanding didn't diminish the impact of the total sum. He'd reached the lowest point of dejection when Mavis called from below.

"Yoo-hoo! Ready for a coffee?"

More expense! Mavis required sugar as well as milk. Could he afford to go on living? Was he the obvious sequential, sacrificial third? Mr Pringle stumbled downstairs.

In her fuchsia coloured jumper with flaming hair above, Mrs Bignell looked like an exotic bloom in his drab hall. She caught sight of his face. "What on earth's the matter now? What's that you're holding?" He gave her the estimate.

"I can't afford to go on living here, Mavis."

"I always said you should move, this place is far too big . . ." She reached the last line and laughed. "My godfathers! They must have seen you coming."

"But I cannot ignore the leak!"

"Listen, dear, there's a girl comes to The Bricklayers on a Thursday — she's a bit too friendly with some of my other customers considering her husband's away serving in Northern Ireland, but these days standards aren't what they were. Anyway. Her father-in-law's brother — it would have been her uncle if it had been her father if you see what I mean — he's a master tiler. She's phoning him for me and he should be calling round for a drink tonight or tomorrow. With that other business last night, I forgot to tell you."

"Is he reliable?"

"Mrs Wattis was satisfied. He did her bathroom-cum-kitchen extension and you know what she can be like. His name's Clarrie and it'll have to be cash because he doesn't declare it on his income tax." Mr Pringle winced. "I'll put the kettle on shall I? I've just finished giving your larder a good turn out — the mould that was growing behind those tins! I should throw them all in the bin if I were you." But he couldn't afford to be that rash.

Police station. Newton's office

Mullin had worked late into the night on his report. He felt proud enough to see that it went dead centre on Newton's desk, clipped to Ian Walsh's statement. He was about to leave when

Newton himself walked in. There was a change of mood this morning, his boss was brisk.

"Morning, Guv, you're early. We've finally got details of the deceased's bank account and Ian Walsh made this statement last night —"

Newton squashed him flat. "I'll read that later. We're going straight to the studios. You'll need a coat, it's started to rain." On the way, walking briskly, he was more forthcoming. "We've been complete idiots. Think back. What happened on Monday when we told the crew to wait until we could interview them?"

"They took themselves off to watch what Doc Pavis was doing —"

"Exactly. Via the overhead camera."

Newton waited until understanding had reached Mullin. "Is that camera switched on at all times and is it, by some miracle, connected to a recording machine?"

"Oh, Christ! How did we manage to miss that? And why didn't one of them tell us?"

"Questions which have been occupying my mind since the early hours, Sergeant. What do they call the area with all the recording equipment?"

"Master Control."

Newton took the steps to Reception two at a time and was immediately engulfed. Shrieking nymphets strutted and posed as mothers and chaperones fluffed up hair and layers of frilly petticoats. "What the hell . . ."

The security man looked at them grimly. "I'd keep right away if I were you. There could be more blood spilt here today before we're through. It's what's known as an audition — hey, you! Come back here!"

A simpering eleven-year-old with black nail varnish paused, one hand on the studio door. "I was only trying to find the ladies."

"No you weren't. You were sneaking in ahead of your turn. Sit down and wait until your name's called. Yes, gentlemen, what can I do for you?"

"We'd like to interview engineers in Master Control."

"Do you know the way? Go ahead. I should leave the back way when you've finished. There's another bus-load from Corona due here at half past ten."

The peace and quiet of the air-conditioned windowless booths was a relief. In the first, a female engineer watched her monitor, expressionless. On it a toothy child announced, "St Joan's speech from the trial scene by George Bernard Shaw . . . 'Light your fire: do you think I dread it as much as the life of a rat in a hole?' . . ."

The engineer noted down the time-code and asked, "Yes?"

"Good luck," said Newton with feeling. "How many are there?" She checked the recording order.

"Twenty-seven this morning and thirty this afternoon. Were you looking for someone?"

"Who's in charge?"

"Stan. Last booth on the right at the end."

"Ta."

"Makes me glad I'm not a father," Mullin observed cheerfully.

"I am," Newton was curt. "Thanks to her mother, she's already stage-struck at the age of eight . . . Morning, sir. Detective Inspector Newton, I don't think we've met."

Stan had the mole-like complexion of one unaccustomed to daylight. He put the duty roster aside. Behind him, screens showed Wednesday's output at Rainbow Television. In A, another scene from *Doctors and Nurses* was being blocked; Robert was demonstrating how high one of the nurses must hold a hypodermic. In B, St Joan continued to defy her judges and in C, a middle-aged author plugged her latest book vivaciously.

"Yes, Inspector?"

"I was hoping to meet the supervisory engineer who was here on Monday?"

"Sorry. Different shift."

"Perhaps you can answer my question. That afternoon, certain employees of this company were caught observing my officers conduct a murder investigation." Stan sniffed his disapproval.

"So I heard. Our bloke had no business to patch that camera through here."

"It's the camera I'm interested in. Is that normally left switched on?"

"The answer's no. The system's activated once the studios are empty. It means one security guard can keep surveillance without moving from Reception. Otherwise, it's left switched off."

"Damn! It was a long-shot but we were hoping . . ." Light dawned for Stan.

"You were wondering if someone had actually seen the murder take place?"

"Obviously no one did or we'd have been told — at least I hope we would," sighed Newton. "I was also hoping that the overhead camera might have been linked to a recording machine."

"Not during the daytime. Once the system's working at night the guard can start recording via his button if he sees anything suspicious, but we can't do so up here. Another thing — that camera has to be operated manually to make it zoom in — which is what our bloke was doing on Monday. Otherwise, it's programmed on an automatic sweep cycle of the whole floor area. But there might be someone who could help you. See that."

Stan pointed to the author babbling away on C's monitor. "That's the transmission picture but there are three other cameras in each of the studios."

"I don't follow?"

"They remain plugged in throughout the day. Even if they're not being used, you've got a picture of something on the off-air screens, usually the floor." Newton's depression began to lift.

"Do technicians watch the output?"

"Vision engineers look after technical quality. They cut between the cameras all the time to match colour balance, independent of the vision mixer. One of them may have spotted something."

"Where will I find them?"

"In Racks. D'you want me to ask if there's anyone in from Monday's shift?"

"Please."

As he dialled on the internal phone, Stan said with heavy humour, "What you lot want to insist on next time there's a murder, is a slaved camera. Like they have on *Wogan*. A camera stays on him throughout the recording then when it comes to the edit, the director can cut to Terry whenever he needs to. Now, if there'd been a slaved camera following Margarite Pelouse on Monday, you'd have had all her action on a separate tape."

"Have a heart. We'd be out of a job," said Mullin. Newton wondered if Ashley Fallowfield would have the nerve to transmit such a murder and decided, unhappily, that he would.

"I suppose none of the cameras *were* slaved?"

"No call for it on a soap. Hello—Kevin? Stan here . . ." After a few moments' conversation he hung up. "You're in luck. Kevin was in A when it happened. He's in on overtime today."

They left via the first booth. The engineer now had both feet on the desk and was reading a fat paperback.

"Keep an ear open for the phone would you, Stella." Without raising her head, she nodded. Behind her reels moved silently, recording image and sound as the fluffy creature cried affectedly, ". . . the blessed, blessed church bells that send my angel voices floating to me on the wind."

"Is that the same one?" asked Newton in surprise. Reluctantly, Stella exchanged her book for the log.

"Number eight," she replied.

"What's it all for?"

"They need a new weather girl at TV-AM."

On their way up the back stairs, Stan commented, "Engineers in Racks, it's even more boring than our job at times."

"I suppose it only gets interesting once there's a technical problem?" Stan glanced at Newton appreciatively.

"Different from your line. You don't begin until there is a problem. Never a dull moment, eh." Newton remembered endless hours spent at a typewriter.

"There is such a thing as routine."

"If I had my time again I know I'd choose differently . . . here we are." He swung open a sound-proofed door. Inside, the engineer called over his shoulder, "Take a seat. Shan't be a minute," and continued speaking into his desk panel mike, intercutting rapidly. On screen, images flickered like an early film. Eventually the colour stabilized to the engineer's satisfaction. Stan bade farewell and disappeared. Mullin stared at the monitor.

"That's Ian Walsh," he said unnecessarily. Newton detected disapproval. Now that they'd stopped for five minutes, he began to feel uneasy about last night's interview.

"Did Walsh come up with anything interesting?" he asked.

"He claimed Pelouse spoiled his chances with Jacinta Charles. Afterwards he says he sent letters which Pelouse kept and it was trying to get these back which led to the row with her on Monday."

"Where and when?"

"The quick-change tent just before she went to the ICU set. He claims the wardrobe mistress overheard part of it and threatened to blackmail him."

"Bloody hell! Didn't any of them behave like normal people?" Newton exclaimed in disgust.

"Walsh was told by Titmouse that Phelps herself had also been threatening Pelouse."

"One at a time, Sergeant," Newton sighed. "We'll deal with the dreaded Rita later. Did Walsh say whether he'd continued his row about the letters once Pelouse was in that bed on the set?"

"He said he thought about it," Mullin replied, "and actually started off toward the set. Then he remembered he'd have more time later on so changed his mind."

"Did he say whether he saw anyone else?"

"One or two leaving Wardrobe on their way to the corridor set or going to lunch, that's all. We can't ignore the fact that it was Walsh's gown that was covered in blood."

"He's not as stupid as that."

"He's an actor." This was so belligerent Newton closed his eyes. Outright prejudice was the last thing he needed.

"From experience, I would have said they were more perceptive as a breed than the average person," he observed. "They're chameleons, adapting instinctively to any new environment. However frightened Miss Charles was, she was ahead on every question I asked and had thought out her replies."

"D'you reckon she did it?"

"No I don't," Newton said shortly.

Kevin finished his conversation and swung round in his chair. "Sorry to keep you waiting." Newton made the introductions and asked his question.

"Did I notice anything?" Kevin repeated. "Only if the colour temperatures were wrong." Mullin was resentful of Kevin's attitude.

"You mean it wouldn't bother you if you saw someone waving a knife about?" he jeered. The engineer looked at him curiously.

"Why should it? I'd assume it was part of the script." Mullin snorted. "All I remember about that particular scene was that the tracking camera had gone through focus during the zoom-in. I was about to tell Bernard we'd have to do another take when Robert shouted the actress was dead. I realized we couldn't go again," Kevin added unnecessarily.

"D'you think the loss of focus was because the cameraman realized he was taking a shot of a dead person?" asked Newton, interested.

"Not him!" Kevin was scornful. "He wouldn't notice if she'd been dead a week. He's just not used to being asked to track and zoom at the same time, that's all."

"Was there anyone who might have been watching the off-air monitors?"

"Speak to the PA." As he said this they became aware of Pat's voice calling shots through the talkback speakers. "You'll have to wait. She won't be free till the lunchbreak." Newton sighed. He'd begun the day with high hopes, but the burden of a sergeant who couldn't see beyond the end of his nose was dragging him down, nor did he relish tackling Pat Fagan. He asked the next question cursorily.

"So you didn't notice anything out of the ordinary, sir?" Kevin hesitated.

"I heard the start of the barney, of course." Newton and Mullin exchanged glances.

"Tell us more."

"Two of the cast didn't notice they were standing beneath the boom."

"What's that?"

"A great long pole with a microphone on the end. Come this way and I'll show you."

They followed through a door on to a narrow balcony projecting out over the studio floor. Heat and a lack of oxygen

94

rose up to meet them. Newton's view of the tightly packed sets was hampered by the grid supporting the spotlights and when Kevin pointed, he stooped to peer beneath the safety rail.

In the two-bed ward, a rehearsal was in progress: Dr Carstairs moved across purposefully only to be stopped and spoken to by one of the nurses. Above the actors' heads, the arm of the boom was fully extended and the mike twisted back and forth to catch each speaker's words in turn.

As the action continued, Newton saw the shape of boom plus mike silhouetted on the wall behind the nurse and wondered if anyone else had noticed. Suddenly one of the cameramen began pointing accusingly at a lamp. On the next-door balcony the lighting director appeared like a jack-in-the-box and gesticulated. Down below, an electrician reached up with a pole to adjust the black barn doors which shaped the path of the beam. Newton watched, fascinated: the shadow had become even more clearly defined. Impasse?

Perched several feet up on his wheeled platform, the boom operator spoke briefly into his mike. The floor manager raised his hand to stop the angry debate and listened for fresh instructions over his cans.

"Yes, Bernard, understood. Penelope love, could you delay your line until you reach the edge of the desk, to give Sound a chance?" The nurse looked to where he pointed, and nodded. Robert gave a questioning glance to the operator, who in turn gave a thumbs-up. The telescopic boom arm retracted slightly, the silhouette disappeared, the lighting director went back into his gallery and the scene continued.

Kevin pointed to where an unattended boom drooped like a predatory long-necked bird over a darkened set. A mike dangled from the end. "Stand beneath that," he whispered, "and we'll hear every word you say."

They trooped back inside. "It's easily done," he continued. "You think because you're out of sight of the cameras, you can have a private conversation."

"It's true there's no such thing as privacy here except when it comes to murder apparently," Newton grumbled. "So you didn't see anything?"

"I heard Robert scream," Kevin repeated. "It was a shock, obviously, but it's no good asking me which of them did it."

"Who d'you mean by 'them'?"

"Members of the cast, of course. It could hardly be one of us, could it? And by 'us', I mean the crew. We only see the actors on recording days. Some, me for instance, never get involved. Today it's *Doctors and Nurses*, tomorrow, it'll be another show. I don't say I never go on the floor . . . If it's variety, someone big in country and western — I'd go down and talk to them like a shot."

"So who was involved in this 'barney' under the boom and what was it about?"

"I only caught part of it. Your best bet is to ask the sound director."

Programme controller's office

Mr Pringle had begun to feel better ever since Mavis told him about the master tiler. He decided fresh air would be more beneficial than remaining indoors. Reluctantly, Mrs Bignell let him go. As soon as he arrived at Rainbow, he'd given Angela letters to type on Ashley's behalf. She'd been indignant of course, but Mr Pringle had stood his ground. Now the result was in front of him.

"Thank you very much," he was too nervous to point out the spelling errors. "Very nicely typed." Angela didn't bother to reply.

"Here you are, doll. I've dictated mine this morning." Ashley handed her a tape. When she'd gone he saw Mr Pringle begin to correct the mistakes.

"You don't have to put up with that, harte. Call Boadicea back and tell her to redo them."

"It's not necessary. These are appeals on your behalf to various districts in the Revenue, but they are sufficiently legible to be understood."

"Legible! They need to be as pathetic as the RSPCA adverts — let me see." Ashley didn't attempt to hide his disappointment. "'Ere, these are a bit dry, petal. Where's the emotional impact? The taxman's trying to bleed me for seven grand not half a crown."

96

"Nevertheless these summaries of mitigating circumstances are all that is required."

"Let Richard have a go?" Ashley begged. "He's a writer, he knows about pathos."

"I think not. We may have to go cap in hand to the Commissioners. It would be unwise to couch any appeal in over-dramatic terms at this stage, Fallowfield." Mr Pringle now knew the full amount Ashley had failed to disclose. It was essential, in his opinion, to behave with extreme decorum. "You must steel yourself for a possible court appearance if we fail," he warned.

Ashley was enchanted. "I shall wear one of my new mourning suits. The charcoal one perhaps, with the silver birds-eye lining."

"What — suits?"

"The ones you said I could buy because of Margarite."

"By mourning I meant sufficient clothing to wear to the funeral, that was all." Apprehension flooded Mr Pringle's veins.

"I had to have a choice. In this climate, God knows what the weather could be like by then. A couple of suits, one's a summer mohair mix, plus that cashmere coat I told you about."

Mr Pringle gasped.

"Shirts . . . pants, one or two matching sweaters — and the sexiest paisley dressing gown. I'm sure Margarite told me paisley was her favourite colour, and I remembered a black tie," he ended happily. "I've kept every single receipt so the taxman can't possibly complain. Look," he reached under the desk, "I've begun a new file." The Liberty carrier bag was already half full.

Studio A. Sound gallery

The gallery was of a grudging size, full of equipment with barely enough space to move. Newton and Mullin were squashed closely together, between the grams operator and the sound director in front of his mixer desk. Noise from the huge twin speakers reached the threshold of pain but the sound director shouted above it.

"Yes, gents? Come to arrest Nick? Be my guest, take him away." The young grams operator flashed a nervous smile and concentrated on the effects track in his cans. John, big and loud, pulled down his faders so that conversation wasn't a strain.

"What can I do for you?" but Newton was watching the screen. "We're finishing off an operating theatre scene left over from yesterday," John explained. "Not to worry. That's Percy they're cutting up, not one of the cast." He roared with laughter at his own joke.

The dummy's plastic feet were obvious on an off-air monitor, but Newton was interested in the blood oozing out of the stomach. "How do they manage that?"

"Chunks of foam soaked in red make-up gunge. Whoops!" The shot had widened too far showing the nature of the "wound". "All is revealed, as they say." Bernard's plaintive roar came over talkback.

"What d'you think you're playing at, three!"

"Got to keep the customers amused," John grinned, "they love a bit of blood." Such exuberance was an irritant this morning.

"I understand there was an argument between two of the cast on Monday, beneath one of your booms?" Hearing the official tone, John's cheerfulness vanished.

"What if there was? It was private, nothing to do with Margarite."

"We'll be the judge of that —"

"Oh, no." John's mood had changed completely. He'd become a big obstinate man who refused to co-operate. "If you want to know what they said, ask them yourself. I'm not telling tales. All I will say is it was Jacinta and Simon and they weren't plotting murder." He shoved his faders up and gave a derisive smile, "Sorry I can't assist with your inquiries." The sudden level of noise made Newton dizzy. He pushed Mullin ahead of him through the door, out in the passage.

Here the air was stale but at least it was quiet. Newton shook his ears to clear them of the din. "We'll leave them to it. What time do they break for lunch? It's obvious he's not going to co-operate. We can't talk to any of them properly while they're working."

"One thirty."

"Fine. Let's nip back and you can show me Walsh's statement." They set off, following the exit signs.

No money had been wasted on these parts of Rainbow Television inhabited solely by staff. Along this passage were old movie posters where customers had once queued. Superimposed over Clark Gable and Paulette Goddard were later, riper inducements for a clientele of a different calibre. One or two of these posters had angry feminist slogans obliterating the sexist message and made Newton cynical.

"Is this the reason for our violent society, Sergeant?" Mullin was indifferent.

"Sex couldn't be the reason for knifing a seventy-year-old, could it?"

"God knows. There has to be a reason even if we don't yet know what it is. In this place I've got a feeling anything's possible."

They went down concrete stairs, along another, narrower passage with make-up and wardrobe rooms leading off, linking it to Studio A. At the first open door, they saw faces peering into mirrors. A little further and actors were hastily changing with Rita ordering them not to drop costumes on the floor. The last door led to what was obviously an equipment room with spare pedestals, dollies and lamps. It was dim in here and the studio beyond, bright by contrast. Newton paused. He and Mullin stared at the back of one of the sets, canvas and wooden flats lashed together, supported by braces and stage weights.

As they watched, the harrassed call-boy tugged at the further door. They heard him shout, "Sorry about the howl-round," before it slammed shut, cutting off their view. Red signs flashed a warning along the passage: ON AIR.

"I reckon this was the route the killer used," Newton said, quietly. "This would be the way to both the ICU and the Wardrobe bin where he or she dumped that gown. Who uses it?"

"Through there leads to the dressing room." Mullin nodded at swing doors ahead, "Up the stairs to the first floor. The cast would be bound to come along here."

"The crew obviously knew of its existence," Newton said. He continued to stand as if expecting one of them to appear. "You know this has to be an inside job. I know we've assumed it was, for convenience, but it doesn't make sense for it to be anything else. Even someone who knew the layout would've had to come past Reception. Their security men are on the ball and anyway, how would a stranger know about any changes to the recording order and whether he'd find the victim alone? I refuse to accept that kind of coincidence. It was one of them and he or she came this way."

Jo poked her head out of the make-up room.

"It is you," she said, smiling, "I thought it was when you went past." She joined them. "That nice Mr Pringle said I should talk to you." Newton raised his eyebrows at Mullin.

"Fallowfield's financial adviser, sir, the elderly chap."

"Uh-huh."

"I did Margarite's make-up on Monday. We gave her an early call because she always insisted on looking immaculate, which meant doing her hair."

"What time was that?"

"Eight thirty." Jo pulled a face. "Jason moaned because he'd had to get up early but we sent him off to fetch the coffees."

"Did something happen?"

"Margarite was upset. I could feel the tension. It was so bad I offered to give her a massage."

"Perhaps she'd had a row with Cornish?" said Newton. It seemed logical; she'd had rows with everyone else that morning. Jo shook her head.

"I don't think so. They seemed happy enough when they arrived and she was all right then. We left her under the dryer in the quick-change tent. Normally we do hair in the main make-up room, but Margarite didn't like people seeing her with the rollers in. You have to remember she used to be a big star." Newton was alert now.

"You mean she was left on her own?"

"Until Jason got back. He came into Make-up and gave out cups to my girls before taking theirs into the tent. I went with him. Margarite was nearly dry so I waited. It was when I began to brush her hair that I noticed the tension."

"Do you know if anyone visited the tent?" Jo shrugged.

"It's perfectly possible. That's our busiest time — everyone to get ready — I don't suppose anyone noticed a thing."

"Ian Walsh," Mullin said quickly. "D'you remember seeing him?"

"No," she shook her head, "and I think I would've noticed him. But he wasn't called until later, he doesn't need more than base and powder."

"What about the extras?" asked Newton.

"We don't make them up unless they're accident victims in casualty scenes. That's only on Tuesdays."

Programme controller's office

Mr Pringle was making inroads on the pile of expense forms. He'd amazed more than one member of staff who, when summoned for interview, took one look and assumed it would be a push-over. To Ashley's surprise, Mr Pringle had already saved the firm a great deal of money. There was a knock at the door.

"Hi," Alix greeted him, "is Ashley about?"

"He murmured something about scenery estimates. I don't think he'll be long."

She handed him a piece of paper. "That was on Angela's typewriter."

In uncompromising style, the note read: "Urgent phone call. Riot at nursery. Back a.s.a.p."

"Goodness," Mr Pringle was astonished, "I thought her infant was only six months old." Alix chuckled.

"Ah, but remember whose genes that child has inherited." She glanced at her watch and found she was holding the photo frame. "Oh, yes, the good news as far as Ashley is concerned — this wasn't stolen after all. I must remember to tell Detective Dexter. One of the crew found it under a radiator." Mr Pringle weighed the silver frame in his hand.

"It's heavy?"

"Yes, it's genuine. Quite a relief that it wasn't stolen after all." As he returned it, the backing shifted slightly. "Blast!" Alix eased the replacement photograph back into position behind the glass. "When we found it, the original photo had fallen out. D'you think this one looks as if she could be Ian Walsh's mum?"

The girl in the photograph was so reminiscent of his beloved Renée, it caught him unawares. For a brief moment Mr Pringle felt unbearably sad. If they had had a son, he supposed the boy would be about Walsh's age.

"Yes . . . quite appropriate."

"I think it's better than the original. That woman looked too old-fashioned. Well, as Ashley's obviously tied up, I'd better get back."

"Was there another message?"

"Yes, but it's rather awkward," she admitted reluctantly. "You remember Bertie who got run over?" Mr Pringle did indeed and Alix immediately apologized. "How stupid of me to forget! The trouble is, he owed me money, out of the float."

"Oh, dear."

"And he'd borrowed a couple of blankets from Drapes. He lived in a ghastly bedsit and he was always complaining how cold it was. We used him practically every week, I thought it was safe to risk lending them. He'd promised to pay me back the money by the end of the month." She sighed. "I'll probably have to refund that myself but I would like to get hold of those blankets, I feel so responsible." Mr Pringle cleared his throat.

"Through an oversight, I have a carrier bag which belonged to Mr Bowman. I'm handing it in at the police station this lunchtime. Would you like me to mention this? I imagine they will be in charge of his affairs until the investigation is complete."

"Would you?" Alix said thankfully. "At least if I can establish a claim on company property. I know Bertie intended returning everything . . ."

"Quite."

"Could you tell Ashley?"

"Certainly, Miss —?"

"Alix. No one uses surnames in television."

Rainbow Television. Staff canteen
It was crowded. Noise bounced off ceiling and walls as Mullin followed Newton, both of them with laden trays, to where the PA, Pat, sat scowling over her notes.

"May we join you?" Newton asked pleasantly.

102

"This won't take long, will it? I've got to check a scene for continuity before we start again this afternoon." He concealed his irritation.

"No longer than necessary, Miss Fagan." Pat sniffed at their choice of menu.

"God, you're not going to eat dead flesh, are you?" Mullin had never considered a kipper in that light before. Newton surreptitiously swallowed a mouthful of chicken Kiev. Pat said earnestly, "They pump them full of hormones you know. They even feed chickens chopped up beaks and claws taken from battery hens which have produced cancer-making viruses —"

"If we could concentrate on our inquiries, Miss Fagan? Would you cast your mind back to what was on the off-air monitors prior to when you heard Robert call out that Miss Pelouse was dead."

"How far back? During scene thirty-nine in the corridor?"

"If that was the preceding scene, yes please. I understand you normally watch all four monitors and would see everyone involved?"

"The vision mixer normally watches the action, PAs call the shots but this time you're right to ask me," Pat was bossily important. "Virginia's bored out of her skull these days. I don't think she'd notice if Jack the Ripper was slitting throats on an off-air monitor." Newton realized this was probably a pleasantry and smiled accordingly.

"In scene thirty-nine, Bernard used two cameras," Pat recalled. "One and three. There was a brief shot on two at the beginning, but apart from that, camera one had the wide shot and camera three, the two-shot." This didn't mean much to Newton or Mullin.

"Weren't there any other shots which would pin-point where everyone was?"

"You can't be extravagant and use all four simultaneously in a soap. You have to be economical because there's always so much material and you're fighting the clock. Bernard moans, all the directors do, because there's no time to polish. You just pray the actors remember their lines and don't bump into the furniture. Television nowadays . . ." and Pat lifted her shoulders to indicate how far standards had fallen. Newton tried another tack.

"I gather there was a spat on Monday, overheard on the boom?"

"Jacy and Simon," she replied without hesitation. "That happened earlier. He's a cameraman. He and Jacy are friendly — were, I should say. Rumour hath it Simon's gone back to his wife," and she bit deeply into her veggieburger.

"What was the quarrel about, do you know?"

"Sorry, I didn't listen. I was checking the running time."

"Do you know what happened after the quarrel?" asked Mullin.

"I'm pretty sure Simon handed over to his tracker which was a bit mean because the next shot on two, the one coming up in the scene with Margarite, was a tricky one."

"Wasn't that where a camera was supposed to poke his lens through the door, after Miss Charles had entered," Newton said slowly. Pat looked at him with approval.

"I say, have you been reading the camera script?"

"I doubt if I'd understand it — perhaps you could explain it to me later. No, it was the floor manager who mentioned that particular shot. In what way was it difficult for an inexperienced cameraman?"

"The angle was awkward. Which is why I guessed it must be the tracker on camera two and not Simon when I saw the monitor. The tracker obviously wanted to practise the move so he pushed his camera over to the ICU set directly I called out he was clear in the corridor, rather than wait until we'd finished the scene."

"You mean — camera two was already in position in the ICU area?" Newton's grip tightened on his knife and fork.

"Yes, outside the door . . . if I had a plan, I could show you." Pat was searching through the mound of scripts and files that accompanied her everywhere. "This'll have to do." She reversed the timing sheet on her clipboard and began sketching the shape of the studio floor. "This is the corridor set here," she drew an oblong in the bottom left-hand corner of the foolscap sheet, "and the ICU roughly diagonally opposite . . ." she pencilled in another square close to the top right-hand corner.

"Show me where the doors are to the rooms," Newton said suddenly.

"What? Oh, you mean Make-up and Wardrobe —"

"And the other one, further along."

"The equipment room? That's practically opposite the back of the ICU." Pat was unaware of the excitement she was causing. "Now, camera two had begun down here." She drew a cross near the corridor oblong. "He took the first shot — of a porter pushing a trolley up and past. As soon as the man had gone through shot, I called out that two was clear, and the tracker then moved his camera across to his next position, over here . . ." Pat's pencil dotted a track skirting to the edge of imaginary sets. "He had to go round the outside, partly because of where he was cabled — roughly from this point in the wall here — but also because of the clutter on the floor. He ended up . . ." She drew another mark between the door of the ICU set and the entrance to the wardrobe room, "here."

"Which way was the camera facing?" Newton forced himself to stay calm. Pat's arrow pointed toward the ICU set door.

"He was ready to follow Nurse Williams when she went through, you see."

"Can you remember — was that door open or closed?"

"Oh closed, naturally." Pat's bossy manner had returned. "Don't forget the first shot of the scene was the track and zoom-in on four, coming round the screens from the opposite direction. Camera two had to wait until four was in a big close-up on Margarite before he could push through that door, otherwise you'd have had the classic situation of two cameras facing one another."

She began drawing camera four's track, but Newton and Mullin stared at one another. Newton knew the danger of prompting Pat's memory. As casually as possible he asked, "So camera two was already there, outside the ICU. You could see the door on his monitor, could you?"

It was so simple: the murderer had to have walked into the eye of the lens when leaving the set on his way to Wardrobe to dump the gown. Pat shattered the illusion.

"Of course camera two didn't stay there," she said crossly. "The poor tracker hadn't even time to practise his move because the porter knocked the wall over and we had to go again in the corridor set, didn't anyone tell you? I shouted to two to get back to his original position as soon as I saw that happen." Mullin avoided catching Newton's eye.

"He had got as far as the ICU set though hadn't he, before you called out?" Newton implored. It was a last ditch hope but surely fate wasn't that unkind? Pat frowned in an effort to remember.

"I watched his monitor, to see if the shot changed. As soon as I saw his lens tilt down I knew he was on his way back."

"So he had stopped, however briefly? What did you see the moment before the lens tilted, or would the tracker himself remember?" Newton ignored the dangers of alerting her now and his voice was sharp. Pat sat up straighter.

"The camera wasn't focused up, it was fuzzy, and the tracker was marking up his position on the floor so no, I don't think he would. There were people dashing in and out of Wardrobe because it was nearly lunchtime. The company doesn't let anyone leave the premises wearing costume. I spoke to the call-boy, to tell him not to let anyone get changed —"

"Who? Who did you see?"

Pat stared into the distance. "I remember hoping everyone had heard we were about to do the corridor scene again," she muttered. "There were two or three extras, one in a porter's uniform —"

"Anyone dressed as an anaesthetist?" asked Mullin before Newton could stop him. Pat looked interested.

"Oh yes, that's what the killer wore, didn't he? Rita told us." She saw their expressions. "You can't stop Rita gossiping, no one can."

"Did you see anyone else, Miss Fagan?" Newton said urgently. "Was Jacinta Charles in position for instance?" He knew she hadn't been, it was clutching at straws.

Pat shook her head emphatically. "No. The only member of the cast was Ian Walsh. He wasn't in the scene with Margarite. The stage-manager had told those who weren't needed to go and it looked to me as if he was on his way out."

"Was there anyone else besides Walsh?" Out of loyalty to Jean, Newton couldn't accept that any actor had been as stupid as to kill wearing his own costume.

"Actually . . ." the bossy voice was momentarily uncertain.

"Yes?"

"It was while we were still doing scene thirty-nine — I suppose

106

Margarite was being stabbed round about then, ghastly thought! There was a lot of noise and hassle, rebuilding the set, etc. But when we came to do take two, something was bothering me then. The policewoman asked me if there was anything we could remember. I said yes but unfortunately I hadn't made a note at the time." Pat was obviously annoyed at her own inefficiency. "I'm afraid I simply haven't had a moment to look at those particular takes on Monday's tape and see what it was." Newton pushed his plate away.

"It'll probably come back." He'd felt deflated. It wasn't important; no one involved in the corridor scene could possibly have killed Margarite Pelouse.

"We do the edit on Friday," Pat told them. "Once I see the shots, it'll come back to me, don't you worry."

Newton was sombre on their return to the incident room. He'd gone through Walsh's statement, trying to filter it of Mullin's prejudice, but now he was half-inclined to wonder if the sergeant wasn't right. Murderers weren't always clever. He gave himself a mental shake and took hold of common sense. "I'm damn sure it wasn't Walsh," he said aloud. "Why kill because of a few old love letters?"

Police station. Entrance desk

Mr Pringle made several discoveries while waiting his turn; the first was that shop-lifting was on the increase judging by interesting conversations he overheard, the second that drunks could make life extremely unpleasant for innocent citizens waiting to hand in property. Eventually, the desk sergeant took pity on him, but was brusque over the request for an interview.

"I've no idea where that particular officer could be, sir. Probably at lunch. Is it important? I'll see that he gets this bag." Mr Pringle was conscious of his promise to Alix.

"There are certain matters —"

"Tell you what, why not give him a bell during the afternoon. You might be able to clear it up over the phone." It wasn't satisfactory but it had to do.

7

NORMAL LABOUR

Police station. Incident room. Wednesday afternoon
There was a sense of purpose now; information was flowing in,
enough to keep both computer operators occupied. Gradually
Margarite Pelouse's personality and precise details of how she
spent her final hours were being put on record after being
painstakingly checked. Doreen Dexter finished her conversation, hung up and went across to Newton.

"That was a report just in from Swansea on a possible match
with the hit and run in Lexington Street, Frank."

"Oh, yes?"

"Ford Capri, desert beige, registration MMB 874 S. Last
registered at a garage in Finchley."

"Keep me informed."

"Will do."

"We're about to check the video against the studio cassette."

She followed him to a cubbyhole off the incident room where a
group were tightly packed round a television and video recorder.
Newton took the only chair and picked up the control box. In
silence they watched Scene-of-Crime's meticulous coverage of
the ICU set, the adjoining area and comprehensive angles of the
victim herself. While Mullin changed the cassettes over, Newton
asked, "Any comments? Any fresh thoughts now you've all seen
it again? Above all, can anyone come up with a motive?"

"The victim looked almost undisturbed," DPW Mackenzie
summed up what many of them felt. "I thought so the first time I
saw her. It was as if the make-up girl had just finished arranging
her hair on the pillow."

"She can't have moved more than a fraction," Dexter agreed.
"When I asked the stage-manager, she said that from memory,
Pelouse was exactly where they left her. I was wondering . . ."

"Yes?"

"Did Pelouse assume they'd begun to 'block' the scene? She was supposed to hold her position throughout, eyes closed. If she was convinced a rehearsal had begun, her instinct would be to remain perfectly still."

"Which implies trust in the killer — but then we know that already," Newton was thinking aloud. "It also means it could be one of the crew."

"If an electrician told the victim he was adjusting a lamp," suggested DC Blaney eagerly, "she'd hold her position for that. She wouldn't worry if he started moving about."

"Until it was too late, you mean? According to Doc Pavis, the killer was probably at the head of the bed when he leaned over and pressed down hard. After that, it would only take minutes before he'd finished her off. She didn't struggle, presumably because she'd been taken by surprise or because the first blow incapacitated her."

Newton looked round as he said this. It still bothered him that Margarite Pelouse had lain quiescent. He hoped one of them would argue or suggest an alternative theory, but no one did.

"The killer rearranged the bedclothes," DPW Mackenzie pointed out. "He must've pulled them back to stab her and then covered her up again, that would have taken time."

"True, but the whole business didn't take more than approximately two minutes from start to finish. I timed Pavis and his assistant going through the motions at the autopsy." Newton frowned. "I'd hoped we'd cut down on the possibilities rather than open up a new can of beans. If we have to start making inquiries of every single member of the crew . . ." he sighed, the dark eyes becoming increasingly depressed. "However, let's not get too down-hearted. We'll take a look at Rainbow's version."

He spooled forward to find the start of the ICU scene, but other images rushed past and he stopped the tape. "This must be the famous corridor where the wall got knocked down. Might as well see for ourselves who was involved. Call them out, Sergeant, we can cross them off as we go." Mullin began identifying the cast.

"That's the floor manager shouting 'action' . . . here comes the porter — all of these are extras."

The shot changed. We're on camera one now, thought Newton. An inexperienced tracker is shoving camera two's pedestal round the back of the sets to where Margarite Pelouse is being murdered . . .

"That's *Dr Nettleton* coming to meet his ladylove *Nurse Simmons*," Mullin continued, ". . . this is where the porter loses control . . . trolley goes one way, he goes another — and crash! Oh, thanks." Newton had pressed the Hold button. Mullin tapped the glass screen.

"From left to right, we can eliminate Robert Wilkinson — he's *Dr Carstairs*, Corinna Pendlebury-West — *Nurse Simmons*, Kenneth Formby — *Dr Nettleton*, and Penelope Pears — *Staff Nurse Hodges*."

"Shouldn't we also cross off the extras?" DPW Mackenzie asked.

"Good thinking, it'll save time if we do," Newton agreed. "Anyone know who they all are?"

DPW Dexter bent down and named those she recognized. At the finish, they began comparing lists.

"As far as the cast goes, we're left with Ian Walsh, Jacinta Charles and Melinda Starkey — who's she?" Newton asked.

"She plays a sort of cleaning lady but we can forget her," DPW Mackenzie told him. "At first we had her down as one of the three who hadn't returned after lunch on Monday. We then found out she wasn't called until that afternoon and according to her agent, spent the morning auditioning for a situation comedy at Thames."

"Did you confirm?"

"Not with Thames, sir, but I asked Rainbow's receptionist and she was positive Starkey didn't arrive until three p.m. which tallies with the book showing when the dressing room key was signed for."

"Fair enough."

"There were two minor parts," Mackenzie went on, "a stunt driver and an ambulanceman. Neither were required until today. I haven't finished checking but so far their alibis stand up."

"That leaves us with the hoi-polloi." Newton nodded to Dexter, "Have we accounted for all of them?"

"There were twelve altogether, all with the same eight forty-five a.m. call on Monday. I make it ten we've seen in the corridor, but would you mind going back to the beginning, sir. I'd like to go through them again."

"Why don't we look at the second version, when the wall stayed up?" But when Newton spooled forward all they saw was a brief glimpse of a VTR clock before the tape went blank. "Hello, didn't they transfer that version?"

"We can find out by looking at the time-code," said Mackenzie. "The PA explained. It's the way they keep tabs on what they've recorded. If you go back to the start of the first version, I'll show you how it works."

Newton pressed the rewind button until he reached the original VTR clock.

"That's for visual identification, like the clapper board in films. The call-boy fills in the details. As you can see he's written, Ep. 27, scene 39, take 1. But the time-code is linked to the actual time of day; it's those figures at the bottom of the screen and it's laid on the recording tape as a guide."

". . . 12.58.48," said Newton, reading them off. "So that's the exact moment when they began recording this scene."

"Yes, hours, minutes and seconds. The PA notes it down at the start of each piece of action. If there are interruptions, if the scenery falls down for instance, or the actors forget their words, she notes the restart time. That way, she knows each correct section to use when they edit the scenes together."

"Uh-huh. You're not thinking of moving into the media, are you?"

"No thanks," replied Mackenzie firmly. "All that hysteria! Give me a nice quiet murder any time." Newton was about to comment, but changed his mind. He spooled through the blank tape until he found the VTR clock for the ICU scene. "The time-code now reads . . . 13.27.29. Is that correct?"

"Absolutely." She sounded pleased, "It confirms everything we've been told. It must've taken about two minutes for the camera to do that tracking move before Robert noticed the blood and, after Bernard had stopped the proceedings, pull back the bedclothes. Pat said she glanced automatically at the clock

111

because they were due to break at 13.30.00 on the dot. When she realized how close they were to an over-run, she called a lunchbreak. It all adds up."

"But look here, it means that Pelouse was stabbed between 12.58 and 13.27 — forget the seconds — which is far longer than we first thought. Over twenty-eight minutes in fact. Not that the killer would know beforehand, he couldn't count on the porter ramming the wall."

"He could assume ten minutes with safety," said Mullin. "He'd know approximately how long it took to get one scene recorded and another one started."

"If he was familiar with television, he would. Even I'm beginning to understand why it takes forever to make three half-hour programmes. However, let's finish our previous exercise before we speculate further." Newton pressed the start button and allowed scene thirty-nine take one to trickle through frame by frame. "Your turn, Dexter." She resumed her check of the extras.

"Porter with trolley — C. Barnes . . . dogsbody in brown overall — W. Pettit . . . porter going across at the back — B. Bowman."

"Is he the one who got run over?"

"Yes, sir."

"Carry on."

"Group of lady visitors miming excited chatter —"

"How phoney can you get!" muttered a constable.

"If you ask them to speak or if one of the cast speaks to them they're no longer extras but walk-ons and you have to pay them more," Dexter said solemnly. She ignored derisive laughter and called out the names until she said finally, "That's it, ten extras. We're left with two females we haven't yet seen which is correct because they weren't needed in the corridor: I. Fanshawe and B. Thorpe."

"Right . . ." Newton rewound the second cassette and stood up. "This afternoon I want those two interviewed." Dexter and Mackenzie nodded. "I also want to talk to Cornish again as well as Henry Titmouse and Rita Phelps. Separately."

"What about the stage-manager?"

"Thanks for reminding me, Sergeant. The rest of you, I want every member of the crew double-checked for that twenty-nine minute period, 12.58 to 13.27 — OK? That includes sound-men, cameramen, engineers, lavatory cleaners, electricians, the lot. Especially anyone who went in or near Studio A equipment room. As we seem to be no nearer establishing a motive, concentrate on those practical jokes we've been hearing about — the deceased may have unwittingly picked on a sensitive flower among that bunch. Oh Blaney, that cameraman, Simon someone or other. I want to know all about the quarrel and why he left his tracker to operate camera two."

Blaney looked pleased to be given the responsibility. Newton stared at the rest of the glum faces. "Get started. And keep smiling. It shouldn't take you much beyond midnight."

Back in the incident room he and Mullin paused by the Actions board. "Next meeting at four p.m." he said and Wicander nodded. "What's that?" He nodded at an easel supporting a large white board. Pinned to it was a familiar looking sheet of flimsy paper.

"It's an enlarged copy of Studio A floorplan for the current episode of *Doctors and Nurses*."

"I can see that," Newton said, miffed. "What I meant was — why?" The receiver came and joined them.

"When we saw it was a cast of thousands, Frank, we thought this might help. I've been listing Monday's events chronologically, see." He held out the foolscap sheets for inspection, "Based on everyone's statements and cross-checked of course. We're just about to see if that corridor scene tallies, time-wise."

"And does it?" Newton waited until Wicander finished and looked up with a smug smile.

"To the second! And now, on the floor plan, we can update the information." He moved to the easel and began to write in a tight, neat script. "We can plot everyone's move minute by minute." Flags marked where cast and crew had stood.

"Why not use colour-codes? Tie them in with the carousel cards. Those we've eliminated in green, those we should concentrate on in pink or something. It'll give a clearer picture."

"Good idea."

"Can you also show diagrammatically who moved where and when? That could be useful."

"No problem."

"Thanks." We're getting there gradually, Newton thought. There was a familiar feeling of increased energy now that a pattern was emerging. He turned to Mullin. "Has the bank come up with anything?"

"The manager was cautious but he used the word 'healthy' and said there weren't any unusual withdrawals or deposits apart from intermittent payments to Jason Cornish during the last six months. He reckoned those didn't add up to more than three grand, including gifts, which was about what she usually lavished on her young men. 'Average expenditure', he called it." Mullin gave a coarse laugh, "I thought I might look for a rich widow lady when I got back to Leicester, Guv. To supply life's little luxuries!"

Newton's wintry expression quelled any desire to make further pleasantries and Mullin returned to his notes.

"It appears Pelouse was given good advice when she was making big money, thanks to Alfred Barker. Her house is a freehold, near Harrods. The bank manager estimates it's worth over a quarter of a million at current rates."

"Now I find that very interesting," Newton said softly. "Who inherits?"

"The Will's out of date, made during her marriage to Willie Henderson, leaving him everything. They lived there of course, but he left when they divorced. According to the solicitor Pelouse was stubborn and refused to make a new Will."

"Don't tell me we've stumbled on a motive at last! Wasn't it friend Willie who telephoned Ashley Fallowfield to check the news of Pelouse's death? Does he know of his inheritance?"

"The solicitor claimed he'd had difficulty contacting him." Newton groaned.

"If Henderson's disappeared while we've been twiddling our thumbs . . ."

"Nothing like that," Mullin reassured. "He's on tour. York, I think his wife said. There was no hint he wouldn't be coming back."

"I want to talk to him but I don't fancy traipsing up north. Find out if he's expected home on Sunday."

"Yes, Guv." When Mullin was out of range, Newton demanded of the incident room at large, "When will someone tell that burk not to call me Guv?"

"We already have," Wicander, pentel poised, smiled blandly, "but Mullin insists you're more chummy than we always thought."

Programme controller's office

Ashley was restless. Rainbow's consortium had suddenly become concerned about their investment. It had taken much coaxing before Ashley could persuade them of the publicity value of the murder. He hadn't bothered mentioning Bertie Bowman's accident. That hadn't made the nationals and with a bit of luck, would soon fade from everyone's memory.

Thought of Bowman prompted him to say, "I've a favour to ask, harte?" Mr Pringle looked up from the latest set of expense claims.

"Yes?"

"You know those blankets? Alix has phoned the policeman investigating Bertie's accident. They've already checked the bedsit and said there's no reason why we shouldn't pop in and collect them ourselves. But the copper insisted they'd only hand the keys to someone responsible and Alix is tied up."

Mr Pringle's own call to the same officer had been brief. The man thanked him for handing in the carrier bag, asked if he wished to add anything further and when Mr Pringle hesitated, thanked him again and rang off. But then it hadn't been a matter he found easy to discuss over the phone and now, despite being nothing more than a witness, Mr Pringle didn't seem able to break free of the nightmare. "Will it be obvious which the blankets are?"

Ashley shrugged. "They'll be the same as the ones in the studio sets."

Nevertheless Mr Pringle was unhappy. Blankets, bedlinen in general, had no identifying characteristics apart from a tendency to burst out of cupboards when he wasn't looking. He'd only to

115

tug at the bottom item in any pile for the whole lot to take umbrage. As for being certain which items he was entitled to remove from a dead man's estate . . . ?

"Perhaps, if my friend Mrs Bignell could accompany me," he suggested, "she is remarkable at finding things." Ashley remembered Mavis from Bath & Wells days, flamboyant and jolly, his type of lady. He cheered up immediately.

"Tell her to grab a taxi and come straight over. I'd love to see her again."

"Alas, that will not be possible. Wednesday mornings she visits the hairdresser. Perhaps some other time?" Ashley had an inspiration.

"Tell Mavis to put on her best frock and we'll go tea-dancing tomorrow at the Ritz." For Mr Pringle, duty always took precedence over pleasure.

"Thursday evenings she is in attendance at The Bricklayers. She may not have the energy for two social engagements in one day."

Ashley stared. "You just tell her the Ritz and I'll bet you a fiver she manages it."

Female extras' dressing room
Interviews with remaining members of cast and crew would, it was agreed, be done at the studio to avoid further interruption to *Doctors and Nurses*. DPWs Dexter and Mackenzie worked their way through the eight of the ten extras and were confronting the remaining pair.

Sylvia Mackenzie had a sinking feeling she'd drawn the short straw this time. During their long wait, these two had titivated themselves, but Iris Fanshawe, the doyenne, had taken it to excess: purple laden eyes, blusher which stretched from ear to chin and red lips which smudged every time she patted them. What was worse, the woman was unable to give a straightforward answer to the simplest question.

"I'm afraid I can tell you very little about Margarite Pelouse. A great artiste, of course. Magnificent. Now, Bertie Bowman I knew from the old days in theatre." The police officer tried to disguise her impatience.

116

"It's Miss Pelouse we're interested in, Miss Fanshawe, and Monday morning in particular. Mr Bowman's accident is being dealt with by another department who will contact you themselves if they think it necessary." Iris put a hand to her brow in an effort to recall Monday's events.

"The first scene that morning I was a hospital visitor, then a sister carrying an unmentionable object into the sluice room. Two scenes later, I did a cross-over when Dr Watkins, that's Ian Walsh you know, opened his bedsit door. I wore a mackintosh for that although I cannot think why since the lighting outside the window indicated that the sun was shining." Sylvia tried to bring her back to the matter in hand.

"What happened during the corridor scene?"

"I wasn't needed for that. The call-boy told me I was free to go to luncheon but I remained at my post," Iris gave a melodramatic jerk of the chin at Beryl Thorpe, "unlike some I could mention."

"Where was that?"

"Pardon, dear?"

"Your post?"

"Up here of course."

Beryl Thorpe heard and was annoyed. "Iris will insist I sneaked off but I never did," she muttered to DPW Dexter. "I heard Robert say all those who weren't involved in the corridor scene could leave so I asked the call-boy what time they wanted me back and he said not until half past two which meant I could go to Marks & Spencer."

"We knew one another at Colwyn Bay," Iris gave a sad smile and shook her head over past glories.

"I'm sorry?"

"Bertie Bowman and I. Such a gifted artiste. Such a tragedy."

"Yes, very." DPW Mackenzie cursed silently as Iris Fanshawe set off once more down memory lane.

"Such a sensitive soul!"

"Monday lunchtime, Miss Fanshawe. You said you decided to go to the canteen for a coffee?"

"Luncheon is normally such a social occasion in here, you see. But by two o'clock when no one had turned up, I took myself up to the fifth floor canteen — it's more a restaurant actually — but as soon as I came out of the lift someone told me the dreadful news — "

"Who?"

"Oh, I can't tell you his name. One of those little men who deal with the lights. I was stunned. In shock."

"At two o'clock you said? A man was already on the fifth floor telling people? Try and remember a bit more about him."

There'd been plenty of time by then but the police wanted to know who'd been first with the news. Iris Fanshawe's eyes bulged with reproach at the lack of sensitivity.

"I cannot be expected to remember every single detail, I was too upset! I came straight back here to recover. If only we'd heeded the vibes! They were so bad on Monday morning, I almost walked out of the studio. I *knew* something terrible would happen. I was right."

"How were they on Tuesday when Mr Bowman had his accident?" The policewoman couldn't resist asking.

The former artiste gazed at her stonily, "If it was in the stars there's nothing you or I could have done to save him."

"So when you got back, Miss Thorpe —"

"At twenty-five past two —"

"There was no one in this dressing room?"

"No. A policeman said I was to come up here and wait, and I was the first one back. Everyone else arrived within minutes of course, because we were due back on camera at two thirty but *she* was one of the last." Beryl Thorpe nodded in Iris Fanshawe's direction.

This was said in a whisper which Iris couldn't hear; she turned and gave her friend a fulsome wave.

"Isn't this exciting!" Beryl Thorpe responded gaily.

"Like *The Equalizer*! Except you don't look a bit like Edward Woodward," she assured DPW Dexter.

On their way downstairs the detectives compared notes.

118

"If Fanshawe says she came straight back . . . and Thorpe claims no one was there at twenty-five past, one of them's lying." Sylvia shrugged irritably at something so trivial.

"I suppose la Fanshawe could've been in the loo. Not that she'd admit to having such vulgar bodily requirements." She glanced impatiently at her watch. "I'll have to come back and ask, I'm due at the dentist in quarter of an hour."

"D'you want me to —"

"No, it's OK. I've got to come back anyway." Sylvia began to hurry.

"I suppose it could be Thorpe who's lying although she struck me as being truthful."

"Fanshawe didn't," Sylvia called decisively, "and she drinks. You should have smelt her breath!"

"Perhaps that's where she went Monday lunchtime, to recover from the shock?"

"More than likely!"

Mavis's warm voice made Ashley chuckle. "Yes, I've had my hair done, dear, but it's my feet. If I'm to enjoy myself I need to have those seen to as well. Did you mean it, about the Ritz?"

"Definitely."

"Aren't you lovely! I've always wanted to go there."

"Tomorrow?"

"Thursday? Why not. Mr P's ever so worried because of the cost."

"It's my treat!"

"That's what I told him. And, I said, Ashley wouldn't invite us if he couldn't afford it. Besides, I said, he needs cheering up with people getting themselves killed all the time."

"Only two so far," Ashley protested.

"I wonder who'll be number three. Shall I come to the studio?"

"Yes. I'll order the limo to take us there." Mavis squealed with delight.

"Wait till you see my party dress, Ashley. Pink with red roses — I've been dying to wear it."

Studio A. Casualty area set
The atmosphere in the studio was tense; the stunt car driver,

119

recalled to say a line necessary for the rewritten plot, was fulfilling their worst expectations. Robert did his best to translate Bernard's temper.

"If it makes life easier, Terry, we can split the sentence and do it in two takes," he said gently. The driver sweated heavily.

"They never told me I'd have to do any words."

"Don't worry!" Robert was hearty, "Relax. You're doing very well indeed. We'll try it again, shall we? In your own time." Sliding out of earshot, he murmured into his radio mike, "Leave the tape rolling, Pat, we'll keep on till he gets it right."

"Where's the camera?" the driver called anxiously.

"Behind you, Terry. Don't worry, we're shooting over your shoulder. Ready, Ian?"

Dr Watkins moved into position facing the lens. The man glanced behind to check. "So no one can see me?"

"All we see is Dr Watkins's face as he listens to what you're telling him. And cue . . ."

In his office, Ashley bade Mavis farewell and hung up. He watched Studio A's output resignedly. Bernard was right, the driver was hopeless, but Ian Walsh reacted as if hearing the words for the first, not the sixth time.

"The patient spoke to you, before she went into a coma?"

"Yes, doctor."

"What did she say?"

"She said . . ." But the driver dried once more. Bernard screamed over talkback.

"Give him the script. Go in tight on Ian, three. Let the stupid ponce read the line, we don't have to see him do it."

Tactfully, Robert reinterpreted. "If you'd like to hold the script, Terry, we won't be able to see it on camera." The man wiped perspiration from his eyes.

"It's so hot . . . I'm a driver, I'm not really an actor."

Up in his office, Ashley said caustically, "We'd guessed that much, petal."

In the control room, Bernard yelled, "We'll put it right at the dub."

120

In Sound Control, big John swore, "A bloody miracle worker, that's what you'll need for this lot, mate!"

On the floor, Robert smiled calmly and encouragingly. "In your own time, Terry. Ready Ian? And . . . cue."

Pat noted down the time-code. "On three," she called mechanically, "coming to one hundred and and twenty-one on one."

Studio A. Prop store/interview room
Newton had reinstated his temporary interview room in a further effort not to disrupt *Doctors and Nurses*.

"See if either Titmouse or the stage-manager are free. Tell Blaney to come and see me after he's spoken to that cameraman and I think we should hear Jacinta Charles's version of their quarrel, too."

"Right. Any particular order?"

"Whoever's easiest." Mullin disappeared.

On impulse, Newton went to the real phone and dialled his home number. "Hello . . . it's me."

"Hi." Jean sounded cautious. He wasn't given to calling unless there was a problem. "Are you going to be late tonight?"

"I shouldn't think so. I wanted to ask if it was your day for the library?"

"No, but I can go."

"That play by Congreve we talked about, can you get it for me?"

"I doubt if they'll have it but I'll try."

"I thought I'd like to read it for myself." What Frank Newton really wanted to discover was the secret; which words could enable an elderly actress to seduce a man like Ian Walsh? It wasn't a topic he felt able to discuss with Jean. "It might give me a few ideas . . ." he finished lamely.

"I'll do my best. See you."

"Yes."

The door reopened and Mullin guided in the agitated Henry Titmouse. "Take a seat," he urged.

"It won't take long, will it?" Like everyone else his life was governed by the clock on recording days. "I've got two more gentlemen to see to today as well as Ian. One of them's got to leave early, he's got an appointment —"

121

"Just a couple of questions, Mr Titmouse," Newton was soothing, "out of earshot of Mrs Phelps."

"She'll start on me as soon as I get back," Henry said sadly, "she always does."

"You can say I told you not to talk, all right?" Henry looked doubtful. "The anaesthetist's gown . . . not the one with blood on it, the other one." There was an insistence behind Newton's tone. "You wrote Walsh's name on the collar-band, didn't you?" Mullin looked astonished but the dresser whipped a hand over his mouth which told them everything. Newton didn't react but continued as before, "Was that in order to placate Ian Walsh?" Henry nodded.

"I was going to use a nailbrush to scrub it off as soon as he'd finished with it. Ian fusses if he thinks he hasn't got his own costume, he's an artiste, you see. But I don't know who took his proper gown, honest to God!"

"All right. We know where it turned up. That other gown, is it back on the extras' rail now?"

"Not at the moment," Henry said primly, "it will be later, when Rita does her check. Ian needed it for one of the scenes this morning. I've been moving it around, you see. If an extra needed it, I took it downstairs and then I took it up to Ian's dressing room afterwards."

"You've been doing this since Monday? Without Mrs Phelps noticing?" Mullin said incredulously.

"She thinks we're too frightened to do things like that," Henry giggled. "You've got to think on your feet in a place like this. Costumes go missing all the time. They usually turn up when recording's finished on Wednesday nights."

"So when Ian Walsh found he'd no gown on Monday, you wrote his name in the other one, and you've been using that one gown for whoever needed it for the past three days?"

"Yes. I thought Ian's would turn up as per usual. Not the way it did, of course," he added.

"Did no one else spot what you'd done?" Henry looked uncomfortable.

"Eric knew, he's the other dresser. I nearly got caught out in the corridor scene. We were supposed to have an anaesthetist as well as a porter for that, but Eric dressed both of them as porters instead. Bernard was too busy to notice but Ian might have gone to his dressing room during the lunch hour so we had to leave his gown on the hook in case he looked for it." Newton leaned forward.

"But the one the killer used, the one that turned up in the wardrobe bin covered in blood, that was the one Walsh normally used?"

"Oh, yes," Henry nodded several times, "I knew it as soon as I saw it — it's got a little tear where I mended it. I'd like to know how it got in that bin."

"So would we, pal," said Mullin with irony.

"When did you last see it?" asked Newton.

"Last Wednesday night." There was a slight hesitancy and Newton jumped on it.

"No you didn't — you didn't check the costumes last Wednesday, did you?" Henry began to stutter.

"I was helping a friend out in the West End. His wife's gone into hospital and visiting hours are two to four p.m. He can't get there in the evenings because of the show, so I looked after his gentlemen for the matinée. I came straight back here afterwards. Eric covered for me."

"Rita didn't notice?" Henry gave Mullin a sly smile.

"I was careful, we always are." Newton had a sudden inspiration.

"You used the fire escape, didn't you?"

"You have to otherwise you've got to go past security in Reception." Henry sat, ankles crossed, pink brow uncreased now he'd confessed, linked safety pins glinting on his overall lapel.

"Have you any idea whether Walsh's gown was left on the rail last week or if it was put in the bin?"

"I don't do the washing. Someone else takes the stuff to the laundrette Thursday mornings. I get in early on Mondays to do any ironing. That's when I find if anything's missing."

So the killer could have taken it a week ago, thought Newton, plenty of time to make his plans.

"OK," he said resignedly, "let's hear about these threats you claim Mrs Phelps made."

"Other people heard as well," Henry said indignantly. "When Rita loses her rag, the whole world knows."

"What was it about?"

"When we got the wardrobe form with Margarite's name on it, Rita was in a real tizzy. She started grumbling about making Margarite pay money she'd cheated Rita out of in the old days. Rita used to be a dresser in the theatre."

"Uh-huh."

"Anyway, Rita slipped Margarite a little note in the rehearsal room, asking if she could see her privately. The trouble is, Rita's not all that good at spelling and Margarite made fun of her. Rita got really mad. She hung about until Margarite was alone one day and then shouted what she'd like to do to her."

"Why wasn't Jason there to protect her?"

"He'd gone to fetch their car."

"And what did Mrs Phelps threaten to do?"

"Kill 'er," Henry said happily. "Strangle, I think it was."

When he'd gone Newton asked, "Would anyone kill for the sake of an old debt?"

"Some people have. We'll have to find out how much it was." Newton agreed.

"D'you think it possible that any single person will walk through that door and declare, with hand on heart that he or she did not threaten the life of Margarite Pelouse?"

"If anyone does, we'll know that's the one."

Alix Baxter hurried in but before she could open her mouth, Newton said, "I know. You can't stay long." She smiled and sat down quickly.

"As long as you do, Inspector. They're relighting at the moment."

"Where were you when Robert called out that Miss Pelouse was dead?"

"Outside the ICU door. Jacinta was supposed to enter carrying a kidney bowl and I was waiting to give it to her." Newton remembered Alix Baxter had been among the names Robert had listed as rushing on to the set.

"Did you see Miss Charles at all?"

124

"Not before Robert called out. She may have been there afterwards — I don't remember. It was chaotic."

"Is it normally your task to hand over kidney bowls?"

"No, but I'd sent the propmen off to lunch. We'd all been busy during the corridor scene, lots of props in that."

"I understand some were missing from your cage on Monday morning?"

"I can't swear if they'd gone *before* I checked with Detective Dexter," Alix said carefully. "You heard about the silver frame turning up?" Newton had.

"I'm more interested in the surgical breast knife?"

"I'm almost one hundred per cent certain it was there when I locked the cage the previous Wednesday night. It doesn't get touched until the following Monday morning when I unlock it for the pre-set. We use dummy props for rehearsals and for the tech run on Sunday afternoons."

"And on Monday morning?" She sighed.

"I unlocked at eight a.m. It's an early set and light on this series. I cast my eyes over the cage — it's all I usually need to do. The surgical stuff looked OK. The knives are in transparent bags with little sheaths to protect the blades. We don't do operating or casualty scenes on Mondays."

"No."

"I was more concerned about things which were missing, like the photo frame."

"Quite." He switched subjects. "This quarrel which took place under the boom."

"Between Jacy and Simon. Yes, someone told me about it."

"You didn't hear?" Alix shook her head.

"I was busy. They were in a corner somewhere. It was people in the control rooms who overheard."

"What about visitors to the quick-change tent. Did you see who went in there to speak to Miss Pelouse?"

"First thing on Monday, Jo went in to do her hair and Jason left them to it. Rita took her costumes in."

"Had the quarrel between them been resolved?" Alix grinned.

"You've heard about that? It was more of an unarmed

truce, I think. I caught the end of the row when Rita was spitting like a she-cat. Something to do with a five-pound note."

"Five . . ."

"Admittedly it was years ago when it represented a week's wage for a dresser, but Rita's not one to forget a grudge."

"Did anyone else visit the quick-change tent?"

"Jason arrived back with coffee —"

"Before he returned?"

"The studio was very busy," Alix protested, "people were arriving all the time."

"You don't remember anyone specific?"

"I have two men to help me set over a hundred and fifty props on Monday mornings."

"Understood."

"Nobody was doing anything out of the ordinary," she insisted. "We were all in the usual mad rush to get everything ready."

Which was the nub of the problem, thought Newton.

When Mullin returned from answering a phonecall, Newton said, "I think we'll leave Miss Phelps to stew a little longer. She knows we've heard about the row — Henry's bound to have told her."

"That was the incident room. Willie Henderson's due back home tomorrow. Apparently the play he was in has been cancelled. His wife's just rung to say he'd called to let her know he'd be back sooner than expected."

"That's saved us a journey to York. Well now, why don't you and I take a look at his inheritance, Sergeant? Near Harrods, I think you said?"

8

A LITTLE TLC

No. 3 dressing room. Wednesday afternoon
It was a very small room. A wash-basin in the corner, dressing
table next to it and opposite, a narrow dingy sofa. Jacinta Charles
lay back on this, eyes closed, thankful to be out of the public
gaze.

She'd managed to get through two whole days, nearly three.
Her major scenes were "in the can" and, thank God, technically
acceptable this time. She'd got one more brief exchange with
Staff Nurse Hodges, plus the remaining shot from the ICU
scene. For that, she had to kneel beside the bed and pretend that
she was speaking to Margarite. Jacinta shuddered. "Once that's
over, everything will be all right!" she whispered.

Bernard and Robert had demonstrated how they could fake
the shot in the two-bed ward using an extra hidden under the
bedclothes in lieu of Margarite.

"We'll do it last thing on Wednesday, Jacy," Bernard promised, "and as soon as you're clear, take a couple of days off. We
can manage without you at Thursday's read-through."

Bless him, she thought: courage had its limits and she was
nearly at the end of hers.

A tap on the door brought back tension. Jacinta moved swiftly
to sit in front of the mirror and fiddle with her hair. Her skin was
dry and there were shadows under her eyes. I've aged! she
thought. "Come in."

Ian Walsh went to shut it behind him but she said sharply, "No,
Ian, leave that open. Wide."

"I only wanted . . ." but he couldn't bring himself to say what
he wanted with members of the cast staring in as they walked past
outside.

"You didn't think, did you?" Her tight nervousness filled the space between them. "The police know everything that's going on in this place. How long before someone whispered that you'd come to see me privately?"

"I'm sorry. You're right — it never occurred to me . . . that anyone would even think . . ." He moved closer, lowering his voice to gain a little privacy. "I had to see you, Jacy." She refused to look away from the mirror so he moved behind her chair. "I wanted to be sure you were all right."

"Don't touch me." Her body ached for comforting arms but part of Jacinta's new-found awareness made her wonder if she'd ever feel secure with Ian Walsh again. "If you want to talk, sit over there. Don't come any nearer."

The call-boy hurried past and she called unnecessarily, "Ready for me?"

"Not yet. About ten minutes."

"Fine. So . . . ?"

"I made a statement last night," Ian replied, "I told them I didn't do it." Jacinta didn't speak. "Unfortunately, I managed to put Sergeant Mullin's back up."

"Unwise."

"Difficult to avoid. He's thick."

"Don't be a moron! None of them are. They're waiting all the time to see what we do." This time she swung round and faced him. "If you haven't worked that out, you're very stupid." Ian flushed as though he'd been slapped.

"I wanted you to know . . . I told them I was sure you couldn't have done it." Jacinta's smile was twisted.

"Under the circumstances, gallantry is not what I need. You've probably increased their suspicions."

"I can't do anything right, can I, Jacy? You've made up your mind about that." She wanted to weep, but she knew that would be both weak and a waste of time.

"Just stay out of my life, that's all I ask." A movement caught her eye. Her dresser was hovering in the doorway. "You can come in." Walsh rose. "Thank you for coming to tell me," she said formally. He gave a brief nod.

"Good luck." And that, she thought bleakly, watching him go, is probably the end of that.

Mullin drove down Park Lane and threaded his way into Knightsbridge. He interrupted Newton's brooding silence briefly. "I didn't spot there was only one anaesthetist's gown."

Newton smiled to himself.

"There were two if we include Walsh's, but only one on the rail. I *assumed* when we knew the killer had taken his, that Henry must have had to use his wits with the remaining one."

"I hadn't credited him with having any."

"He's a dresser," Newton reminded gently. "He's dealt with temperamental actors all his life and that means supplying them with costumes, as and when required."

They pulled up a short distance from the mews and Newton absorbed all there was to see and feel. The ambience of superabundant wealth from cars with engines too powerful for their owners' capabilities and laquered elderly women exposing pitiful shanks in the latest fashions. This was where Margarite Pelouse had lived both during her marriage to Willie Henderson and throughout the years since.

"It's a gingerbread house." Mullin's description was apt. It was small, dwarfed by larger neighbours, with a steep roof topped by a weathercock.

A movement at an upstairs window caught Newton's eye; a figure was retreating in the shadows. "Someone's at home?"

"Probably the housekeeper," said Mullin. "According to the solicitor, she's been kept here until Henderson decides what he wants to do." Newton leaned on the bell.

"It looked more like a man to me. If it's Cornish, he's got a nerve, but it'll save us time. I want another chat."

Jason answered the summons and tried half-heartedly to bar their way. "I decided as I was passing to collect my things," he blustered. Newton saw packing cases beside the luggage in the hall.

"What a shame we interrupted, Mr Cornish. However, as we're here, shall we make sure all those things are yours? Let my sergeant have the keys of the house, please."

"I . . . I . . ." but an ageing male model was no match for the man from Leicester. "Hang on! I'll find them for you."

"And the deceased's car keys," rapped Mullin. "That Rover's part of the estate. And whatever else you've absent-mindedly tucked away."

"Where's the housekeeper?" demanded Newton.

"She's not here —"

"Why not?"

Jason turned from one to another at bay as Mullin began emptying the contents of his suede jacket on to the hall table.

"I told her she could take the day off — hey, those are mine. Margarite gave them to me."

Mullin began dividing the objects into piles. "J C . . . J C . . . JC . . ." he murmured, pushing initialled lighter, wallet and filofax towards him. "Gifts, you said?" He managed to imply contempt in every word. Cornish sulked.

"Let's leave the sergeant to carry on, shall we?" Newton suggested. "You can show me over the house."

Jason, reluctant in the extreme, found himself being urged up the stairs. "The living-room's on the first floor . . . dining-room and kitchen are downstairs. Main bedroom and bathroom on this floor . . ." He became nervous when he realized Newton wasn't listening.

Keenly interested in Margarite Pelouse's chosen surroundings, Detective Inspector Newton was disappointed. He'd been expecting elegance, but this was a time capsule reflecting her great days in the theatre. Furniture, lamps and curtains, all lacked the stamp of personality. It was as though, having walked through Heals with a chequebook, she had straight away lost interest.

In the fifties everything had been new, now it was shabby. Thirty-year-old theatre posters hung on bamboo wallpaper. There was none of the memorabilia he'd been expecting, no plants or flowers. "I'm stereotyping her as an actress," Newton told himself, "and when it comes to fresh roses, toy-boys probably aren't that generous."

The living-room stretched across the front of the house. He wandered from one shallow bay to the next, thinking, A quarter of a million quid . . . and there's rot in the window frames! Without thinking about it, he pushed his thumb into the soft

130

wood, and noticed the bureau. There were photographs grouped together on the top.

"She didn't have children, did she?" He knew the answer but the question interrupted Jason's anxious babble. "D'you know who these are?"

"Husbands. Former lovers. That's Willie Henderson."

Newton recognized the professional Englishman. Henderson had found a niche playing second fiddle to various leading men, usually American. It occurred to Newton that he hadn't seen the face lately. As if guessing his thoughts, Jason said spitefully, "Willie's latest play flopped."

"Oh?"

"They tried it out in Liverpool before they went to York. A revival of John Van Druten. The critics slammed it. Margarite was delighted when she read that. She always wanted Willie to fail. She believed his marriage would collapse and he'd come crawling back here. He never did, of course." Jason examined the photograph again. "What appealed to her — Willie was so typically British." He picked up another snap. "This was her first husband. The same type as you can see." The profile was in black and white.

"Was he an actor?"

"I believe so. Margarite always went for the same sort. Barker was the exception. He was tough, gave as good as he got, which might explain why she was so devastated when he threw her out. She was always talking about *him*. Without realizing it, I think he was the only one she really cared about. All the rest, Willie included, we were people she could manipulate." It was a sorry admission.

"Was she very difficult?"

"She was frightened of growing old," Jason sighed. "She never came to terms with the loss of her looks, always demanding to know how beautiful she was, morning, noon and night." He handed Newton another, smaller photograph. "You can see why. This was her at the time of her first marriage."

In the faded snapshot Newton could still make out the vivid face. "She looks so alive!" Jason pushed it back with the rest.

"I wish I'd been around then," he sounded wistful. "That's

131

when she must've been fun." Newton recalled him to the present, to the half-open drawers.

"What have you taken?"

"Not much," defensive yet hopeless.

It was an amateur attempt and Newton shook his head when Mullin entered, waving a shabby mink stole, "Look what I've just found. When were you planning to wear it, Cornish?" Jason drew breath but Newton cut him short.

"For God's sake, it must've been listed on her insurance. Where's your common sense?" The flabby, once-handsome features sagged.

"I've got nothing to fall back on," he whined.

"Try working." Mullin was unsympathetic.

"About the events of Monday," Newton began. Jason looked up, startled.

"You can't believe I killed Margarite!"

"I think you may have contributed to her death by leaving Miss Pelouse unprotected early on in the day." Before Cornish could protest, Newton switched tactics. "What was her mood the previous week, once she'd got the part?"

"I've never seen her so excited, especially when the script arrived. She began changing the lines, to give herself more, you know the sort of thing. After she'd been for a Wardrobe fitting — it was a recording day — she went on to the studio floor to meet the cast, including Jacinta Charles. She was really edgy after that. She kept on about getting her own back, on Jacinta as well as Ian Walsh."

"Why? It was ancient history."

"Margarite was a Scorpio with a sting full of venom. She never forgave or forgot. Jacinta Charles had tried to rake up a bit of the past which Margarite wanted forgotten. Forbidden territory. And Ian Walsh had changed. He kept his distance with Margarite but he couldn't take his eyes off Jacinta."

"On Monday morning, you remained with Miss Pelouse until you went to fetch the coffees."

"Yes."

"How long did that take? Ten minutes? Longer?"

"About that." Cornish was evasive.

132

"About — what?"

"Margarite was being difficult — I hadn't had a moment to myself all week. I needed five minutes to — to make a couple of phone calls."

"Why?" Mullin, scenting a trail, was on the attack.

"That's my business."

"We'll get it out of you Cornish. You'll come back with us to the station and stay in a cell until you talk."

"Was it money?" Newton remembered the incident in the star dressing room, "She must've left her things up on the first floor before she went down to the studio. Were you trying to get hold of her wallet on the way to the canteen?" Jason immediately began to crumple. "What happened?"

"Look, things had been getting worse between us. I knew Margarite was thinking of throwing me out — she owed me something, for God's sake."

"How much did you take?"

"Nothing!" he shouted. "The bitch had locked her wallet in her dressing case instead of leaving it in her bag. She'd got the key for that in her wrap pocket. I only found it after she'd changed into her nightgown for the ICU scene —"

"And then we arrived just as you'd finally got your hands on the cash," Mullin was relishing the memory. "Looks like you're an all-time loser, Cornish."

He might well be, thought Newton, but he's no murderer. "What was the quarrel with Rita Phelps about?"

Jason, exhausted by the outburst, said wearily, "I don't know, some tale about her once asking Margarite to put five pounds on a horse. It was when betting shops were illegal. Margarite kept the money instead and the horse won."

"Five pounds isn't much."

"It was a week's wage for a dresser and the odds meant Rita could have bought a house with the proceeds. That's what she was yelling that day in the corridor: 'I could've had my own home with that money', she kept shouting. Margarite said she'd kept the money to cure Rita of gambling."

"Who do you think killed Miss Pelouse?" Newton asked suddenly.

Caught off-guard, Jason blurted out, "Ian Walsh, has to be."

"Why?"

"Because of Jacinta. He's mad keen. I told you, I've watched them together during rehearsals."

"A few old love-letters and a half-baked affair with Pelouse wouldn't have kept them apart," Mullin said scornfully. "There must have been more to it than that." Jason Cornish looked at him curiously.

"Oh, there was. His career. Why d'you think a really good actor like Ian Walsh is stuck in a soap? After that tour, when Walsh walked out on her, Margarite made sure he didn't get any decent offers."

"How?"

"She threw an end-of-show party, invited agents and producers and arranged for the barman to spike Walsh's drinks. Halfway through, he keels over in front of everyone. She did a great job and mud sticks, but he was big enough to forgive and forget. The first day of rehearsal he came straight over and gave her a big hug, which was decent, considering. That's when I heard Margarite whisper if he so much as looked at Jacinta Charles she'd do something terrible. She never forgave did Margarite, there was always a sting in her tail." Mullin was incredulous.

"Did she have that much influence nowadays?"

"Ian Walsh believed she did. She'd proved she could be poison once — she boasted to me she could pull another trick on him if she wanted to — it doesn't take much to frighten backers. In his shoes, I'd have felt scared. It could be enough to make a man want to kill."

"On Monday morning when you finally came back with the coffees?" Newton pressed him.

"Margarite was obviously upset," Cornish admitted. "When Jo the make-up girl left, I asked what it was. She nearly bit my head off."

"And that's all you know?"

"Yes. I swear it."

"Hmm!" said Mullin.

On the way back to the studio Mullin complained, "That was

fanciful stuff. I reckon if we'd leaned on him we might have got something else."

"I thought what he told us sounded genuine?"

"But not the whole of it."

"We can always pull him in again. He's given us enough for one day. We'll stick to my methods, Sergeant. Slow but sure maybe, but they're closer to the book and I believe, bring better results. If we lean too heavily at this stage, Cornish will clam up out of fright. Tomorrow, he'll probably be ready to tell us a bit more."

Finchley. Garage forecourt
The garage had been built in the 1930s when the exterior had been white with fanciful Egyptian motifs. That was all a long time ago. Thanks to the war there was a cleared space behind, now full of second-hand vehicles.

A police car drove slowly past, pulled round in a tight circle and drew up on the forecourt, blocking access to both pumps.

It hadn't come for petrol and was a complete discouragement to potential customers. The garage owner was beside it before either policeman had opened a door. "Yes, gentlemen?"

"Checking on a hit and run, mate. We think you could have a vehicle that might fit."

"Come inside," the owner invited. "You wouldn't like to park your motor round the back?"

"No, we wouldn't."

The owner recognized the description immediately. "That one's still around, it's not been sold. It'll be out the back unless one of the lads has borrowed it."

"Do you allow employees to use the cars? What about insurance?"

"There's only Brian or Terry. Terry's part-time. Good mechanic when he's not driving for the films. That's what he's doing today as a matter of fact."

"What about the other bloke?"

The garage owner opened the door to the workshop.

"Brian! Come in here a minute."

As they waited, the constable asked, "Did you ever drive that particular car?"

"Nah! Got a Merc. That little motor's all right though. Repossession job. Very low mileage. Taxed, MOT—"

"Not interested, thanks."

"No harm in asking . . . Ah, there you are. These gents want to know if you've robbed a bank, Brian."

Studio A. Prop store/interview room

When told of the lie, Newton decided a formal atmosphere might frighten the truth out of Iris Fanshawe. He had the tapestry throne exchanged for a straight-backed functional chair and sent for her. Sylvia Mackenzie looked on, grim-faced. She saw it as a reflection on herself.

Iris tried to pretend she was playing a part but the man with the mournful eyes hadn't time to waste.

"I must warn you it is an offence to lie to a police officer, Miss Fanshawe." Maintaining one's poise after that was difficult. Iris opened and closed her mouth but nothing emerged.

"You were alone in the female dressing room on Monday lunchtime?"

"Yes, then I went to the restaurant for a coffee."

"I want the truth, Miss Fanshawe." Iris bridled.

"Really! I'm not accustomed to being —"

"You went somewhere else. Where? Was it a pub?" Words tumbled out suddenly.

"Not at first. It's true I needed a drink. Bertie Bowman, a dear old friend —" Newton raised a hand. "I knew he wouldn't mind," Iris persisted.

"He had liquor?"

"A hip flask."

"So you went into the male dressing room and took Mr Bowman's flask without his knowledge?"

"I . . . I . . . ." Newton leaned forward threateningly.

"Who was it told you Miss Pelouse had been killed?"

Outside the canteen, DPW Dexter stopped Alix and asked, "Can you tell me if any of the electricians are about?"

136

"That's easy, they always sit together." She scanned the tables quickly. "Over there, by the window. The miserable looking bunch."

Doreen Dexter made her way across. Six hostile faces stared up at her. "Good afternoon. I'd like to know if one of you spoke to an extra, Iris Fanshawe, about two o'clock on Monday and told her of Margarite Pelouse's murder?"

Iris Fanshawe was clutching her hanky as Dexter walked in. Newton glanced round. "It's all right, Doreen. It wasn't one of the electricians, apparently. Miss Fanshawe has decided to tell the truth this time. Go ahead, Miss Fanshawe."

"Neither of us knew she was dead. All Bertie said was he thought Margarite had had some kind of accident, he'd heard someone say so in Wardrobe but he hadn't waited to find out the details. He was badly shaken even so, which is why we went to the pub. His flask . . . as I said before, there wasn't much left," Iris said hesitantly then went on. "We used the fire escape — it's not a crime — the dressers go that way all the time. And Bertie was in shock," she added tearfully, "we both were."

"Why didn't you tell us this before?"

"It had nothing to do with what happened! If Mr Bowman and I chose to calm our nerves, what business was that of anyone else?"

Gawd, thought Newton. He slumped in his chair.

"All right, Miss Fanshawe, you can go."

"Am I not to make a statement?" Pride demanded that much.

"No thanks, that's it."

Newton ignored her magnificent exit. Outside the door, Iris reached for her powder compact. Despite all that had happened, she'd kept Bowman's reputation intact. He'd died a gentleman and she was responsible. Head held high, she swayed out of the studio.

Inside the room, Newton asked bitterly, "So who else used the fire escape before we got here on Monday?" Neither detective spoke. "According to Fanshawe, Bowman went up to the dressing room for his usual tipple only to find Fanshawe had already drunk most of it. My guess is he then demanded she buy him one at the pub."

"That sounds about right," agreed DPW Mackenzie.

"OK," Newton sighed, "the autopsy will tell us how much of a boozer he was. Go and tell Mullin to wheel in Rita Phelps. I've just about enough strength left."

"There were a couple of messages at Reception," Dexter told him. "The vehicle that may have been used in the hit and run has been located, and remember the drug pusher's landlady — her memory's suddenly improved."

"Better late than never."

"She thinks the victim *may* have had a visitor the night before he fell under the train."

"Great." Newton was cheerful again, "If we pull her in maybe that'll improve her memory even more. You can send in the lovely Rita now but don't either of you disappear because she frightens me."

Surgery on outskirts of Hendon

In his busy life, a patient who failed to keep a special appointment was a pain. The doctor let his temper boil over. "Have you tried his home number, I'm not prepared to wait all night."

"There's probably a simple explanation, doctor," the nurse reproved. "Mr Goodhill was perfectly reliable in the old days, before his daughter was killed. That was before your time of course."

"Is there a note of his number anyway?" There was silence while she checked.

"No, doctor, only a business one. I remember all about him because of that tragedy. His daughter was knocked down at the traffic lights on Hendon Way. Mr Goodhill needed sleeping pills for a long time after that."

"Try and get hold of him," the doctor apologized. "It's time he had that check-up."

At her desk, the nurse dialled and the garage owner answered.

"A.1 Motoring, thank you for calling?"

"I'm trying to contact a Mr Terence Goodhill."

"He's not here today. He's making a film."

"He failed to keep an appointment, could you ask him to contact his doctor's surgery —"

"Give Terry a buzz at home, darlin', we're not in the business of taking messages. 345 3151, OK?" She was left with the dialling tone.

Studio A. Prop store/interview room

Mullin had joined them, but if Rita was intimidated to find herself facing four police officers, it didn't show.

"Mrs Phelps, I'll come straight to the point. What was it you think you overheard in the quick-change tent?" Before she could reply Newton added quickly, "And I don't want any lies."

"As if I would!"

"Good. So?"

"He threatened to kill her, Ian Walsh did."

"So did one or two other people," Newton replied tartly. "Before that, what did he say?"

"He asked her to be reasonable."

"And?"

"He said he was sorry if he'd hurt her feelings before."

"And? Come along, Mrs Phelps, I don't want to squeeze it out of you, it's late."

"You're holding me up an' all," Rita flared. "I've got costumes to check."

"Let us consider your position. When you threatened to strangle Miss Pelouse, had you any intention of carrying out the threat?"

"I'll murder Henry Titmouse!" Venom landed as spittle on the desk top.

"You were overheard by more than one person," Newton assured her. "However I repeat my previous question: what did Walsh say?"

"Some of it I didn't listen to," Rita assumed a virtue she didn't possess. "It sounded like her trying to make him grovel. She called Jacinta Charles an upstart, that's when the shouting started. Ian said she was a — well, you know. The worst name you call people."

"Did Miss Pelouse make any threat?"

139

"She said she'd ruin him and he said she'd tried that once too often and that he'd stop her foul mouth permanently if she so much as tried." Rita looked round triumphantly. "Ian definitely said that."

"And then he left the tent?" Newton deflated her.

"Well, yes, he did."

"Was anything else said?"

"Something about letters but I didn't catch all of it. I'd got work to do." Mullin gave a snort.

"I shall require you to attend the police station tomorrow morning, Mrs Phelps, to make a statement."

"Thursday's my day off!"

"Most unfortunate," Newton said drily. "I would advise you not to repeat anything said in here today." Clasping his hands, he leaned across at her, "Your nephew may be bent, Mrs Phelps. I play it by the book. That could turn out to be even worse." Defiance evaporated.

"Can I go now?" Newton spoke over her head to DPW Mackenzie.

"Check we have the correct address and telephone number for Mrs Phelps."

"Yes, sir."

When they'd gone, Mullin couldn't conceal his satisfaction, "She came through quick enough that time. Are you going to pull Walsh in for further questioning, sir?" Newton felt sour.

"Yes, but not yet." He still couldn't accept that Walsh had behaved so stupidly.

In the programme controller's office, Ashley and Mr Pringle were watching the final scene of the episode on the monitor. Jacinta Charles was in the two-bed ward. Robert was speaking to her gently.

"Bernard's asking if you'd like to go straight for a take, Jacy."

"Could you mark my position, as it's crucial."

"Sure." The floor manager stuck a piece of yellow tape on the floor. In bed, the shape of a body under the covers was all that could be seen. Beryl Thorpe lay inert and tried to imagine what it must be like to be a star.

"Everyone ready?" Robert heard a studio door open and called sharply, "Quiet please! We're about to record." Newton and Mullin froze. "OK, Jacy?" She took up her opening position and nodded. "Roll the tape, Pat."

From where they stood, Newton had an uninterrupted view of the set. It was brightly lit and everyone's attention was focused on it.

In the control galleries, in Ashley's office, far away in Master Control, they watched the shot on monitors.

"Five," Robert repeated, raising five fingers. As Pat called zero, he lowered his hand and nodded silently at Jacinta.

The opening move was awkward in the revamped set, but she managed it gracefully and sank to her knees hitting the yellow mark precisely. Both hands reached out to an imaginary, unseen Margarite Pelouse as she spoke the banal words.

"Don't leave me, mother . . . not now I've found you . . . Please!" Newton felt a pricking behind the eyes as unbelievably, emotion took hold. At the bedside Jacinta bent her head and held the pose perfectly still.

In the control gallery Bernard yelled, "Roll the roller!" and on the far side of the studio, a scene-hand operated the machine with camera four locked off on the shot. The vision mixer super-imposed one source on the other. As the director's credit rose out of sight top of frame, hidden from cameras, Robert tapped Jacinta. She raised her head and this time stared directly into the lens, her face wet with genuine tears, framed in a big close-up.

"Please!" she repeated in a whisper. After about a second and a half the vision mixer mixed from the BCU to Rainbow Television's logo.

"Five seconds . . . Hold for ten," Pat switched off the cue-dot, ". . . three, two, one — thirty black!"

"That's a wrap, thank God," said Ashley Fallowfield.

On the studio floor, Mullin said pointedly, "She's a *very* good actress."

"Which doesn't prove a thing," Newton answered curtly.

Wine bar in Soho
It was becoming a nightly ritual and Mr Pringle was feeling

decadent. "I dare not confess to Mrs Bignell that I now consume two glasses of red wine before returning home."

"Have another," Ashley said recklessly. "We've got something to celebrate. I want to thank you, petal, for reducing those expense claims. Have you any idea how much you've saved Rainbow Television?" Mr Pringle gave a modest smile.

"It's been an interesting experience . . . in the Revenue days, I usually met accountants. Some were most creative, as clever as the criminal fraternity — indeed one or two made the inevitable transition. Their clients I rarely saw, but in these past few days meeting actual tax-payers has been something of a revelation. I'm glad to say I've been able to save money for one or two who hadn't claimed their full entitlement."

"Lucky devils!"

"Alas, Fallowfield, as far as you are concerned, I cannot hold out much hope."

"It's been good while it lasted," Ashley was philosophical because of the wine. "Maybe that appeal you sent will touch their heartstrings." Mr Pringle tried to visualize the Commissioners possessing such organs, and failed.

"Perhaps we should rethink my fee?" he suggested diffidently.

Ashley gave a sad smile. "You're so bloody cheap, that would be a sin."

"There was the occasional employee who told falsehoods, I fear."

"You amaze me."

"It astonished me that they should imagine I was gullible."

"I never thought that." Ashley shook his golden curls vigorously, "I don't employ dumbos. Mind you, I'm glad you've survived. The way you told some of them off I thought you must be planning on sharing a memorial service with Margarite." He lifted his glass, "I wouldn't have dared."

"When it's a simple question of right or wrong," Mr Pringle said solemnly, "there can be no argument."

"If only the EETPU would accept that." They both drank deeply.

"The police have been questioning more of your staff today.

142

From gossip, it appears they now believe the murderer could be an employee."

"I don't see it. I mean — why? Margarite upset people, sure, but not those she depended on. Make-up, Lighting — she was so vain — she never annoyed those who made her look good on camera. Consider it another way: what's the main reason people kill one another?"

"Domestic unhappiness," replied Mr Pringle promptly. Ashley pulled a face.

"It doesn't make sense for it to be Jason. She didn't have any other 'domestic' life. I don't think Ian did it and the police aren't interested in Jacinta. What other reasons are there?"

"Money?" Ashley shrugged.

"Margarite was comfortably off."

"I heard that she'd once cheated Mrs Phelps." Ashley brightened immediately.

"That's right . . . and Rita pops in and out of Wardrobe all the time. No one would notice if she'd got an anaesthetist's gown tucked under her arm . . . Oh, glory be! I hope the police decide it's her not Jacinta." His opinion on cast changes had obviously been revised. "What a great little actress she is, isn't she. Wait till the viewers see those tears — the ratings will soar!"

"But how, by stabbing Miss Pelouse, would Mrs Phelps obtain financial redress?" Ashley thought that merely a quibble.

"Passion," he decided. "Behind those awful teeth lurks a burning desire to get even, and Rita couldn't control herself. Talking of passion, harte, how are Mavis's feet?"

Hendon. 5A Blake Road

He hadn't bothered to put on the lights. Terry Goodhill had lived here so long he knew his way blindfold. He sat at the kitchen table in darkness. A curious passer-by might wonder why the silhouetted figure was so still.

In the hall, the telephone rang for the final time. When it stopped, he unclenched tight fists. Noise made his head reel. His body ached with tiredness yet he was afraid to sleep. The image of Anne returned to reproach him every time he closed his eyes. He craved the numbness pills could bring, but the doctor had refused him. All the certainty Terry had known previously, disappeared. Retribution had brought only madness; God had deserted him. He was utterly alone.

The Newtons' bedroom
Newton wasn't an avid reader at the best of times. He avoided novels because they demanded too much, preferring routine police bumph, facts that had to be learned and stored away.

A play was awkward. You needed to remind yourself who was who, there was no description to help. He'd scribbled: Mirabell = Ian Walsh, Millament = Margarite Pelouse. As for the eighteenth century chit-chat . . . He shifted restlessly. It was past midnight. A pillow slithered to the floor and Jean murmured, "What is it?"

"I don't get it."

"Mmm." She resurfaced. "What don't you get?"

"What it's about chiefly." Jean yawned and stretched. "You said it was better than lovey-dovey." The stretch collapsed as she laughed.

"What's the matter, doesn't it turn you on?"

"I wondered what it did for Ian Walsh."

"I doubt if it was anything sexual. Margarite Pelouse was a great actress. On stage, she probably swept him along, lifted his performance. When it works and you have the audience in your hand, you feel god-like, completely exhilarated. In a way, that's as good as sex."

"Doesn't it disappear once the curtain comes down?" he asked seriously.

"In that instance — Ian Walsh was still finding his feet as an actor — the sensation obviously lingered. He wasn't the first young man to be bowled over by an older woman, especially an actress like that." As usual, Frank Newton was sensitive to any reference to a difference in age. He switched off the light.

"I'll find out what she was really like as a person tomorrow," he said, dismissing the subject. "We're meeting Willie Henderson."

"Did he do it?"

"I've no idea, that's why we're seeing him." He forced himself to mention a topic he'd been avoiding. "This theatre business . . ."

"Mmm."

"If you wanted to go back, we can easily afford a child-minder." Jean Newton stared at the darkened ceiling. She'd hoped her last outburst had been forgotten. Afterwards, in her comfortable home with her daughter, she'd had time to recollect the misery of trying to find work, the agony of failing one audition after another. On his side of the bed, Newton misunderstood the silence and tried to reach her. "I don't want to stand in your way if it's what you want, Jean."

"We'll see," she said evasively. "There's no rush." He understood. Relief was enormous, so was tenderness. He must tread delicately to avoid hurting her pride.

"I forget how dull it must be, stuck at home all day with Emma. Being a father at my age, it's still something I can't get used to, even after eight years."

"You poor old thing!" she mocked. "I'll have you know your daughter can be great company at times."

"Takes after her mum, then."

"Shut up and go to sleep." But she snuggled up so that he knew she didn't really mean it, not yet.

9

TEMPORARY DRESSING

Small flat in Hampstead. Thursday morning
The Hendersons must have bought the place years ago, Newton decided, when the area was inexpensive. He was sure neither of them could afford to now. Not that the small rooms lacked style, but there was an impoverished feel, plus a lack of central heating.

He and Mullin looked uncomfortably large. It was Mullin's fault, Newton decided unfairly, he stuck out like a sore thumb. He waited until Melissa Henderson sank gracefully on to the sofa; from across the fireplace he could sense her tension. Willie took up a position beside her, one arm negligently resting on the mantelpiece. For Newton, it looked theatrical, but no doubt they were unconscious of it.

Willie Henderson had played second lead when television pictures were in black and white: even so it was a surprise to see the silvery hair. Tall, in tweeds and a waistcoat, he was the epitome of an advertiser's countrybred Englishman. Melissa, with her elegant casualness, was the perfect foil against faded chintz. Frank Newton wondered if either of them had ever lived anywhere but London.

"I'm awfully sorry I can't help you, Inspector," Willie Henderson sounded relieved rather than apologetic. "I left York very early this morning and arrived half an hour ago, that's when Mel told me you wanted to see me." Out of habit, he smoothed one hand over his hair in a gesture that had once enchanted matinée audiences.

"You were appearing at the theatre in York on Monday, I believe?"

"Not exactly." Willie hesitated. "We'd opened there last week. The original plan was a ten day run in York following a week in Liverpool. But local reviews in both places were terrible and then the Sundays crucified us. That's when the management decided to cut their losses. I'm sure business would've picked up . . . one has a certain loyal following in the provinces, but there you are, you can't argue with the angels."

"Let me get this straight, Mr Henderson. You've been away three weeks altogether. You performed throughout last week in York and finished there on Saturday night?"

"That's right. Although we didn't know then that it was the final performance, of course. We thought we'd be playing there from Monday to Wednesday of this week as well, returning to London today."

"When was the decision made to terminate the run?"

"Monday morning."

"In York?"

"Sort of. There was a discussion over the phone. We had three main backers, one in York and two in London. Then there was myself. Mel and I had invested our savings . . ." He glanced at her. "I don't know whether I should have told you that."

"It would have come out sir, eventually."

"Yes, I suppose it would." Willie Henderson's open countenance was guileless, "The form is that I tell you everything even if I think it irrelevant?"

"That's right, sir. And were you in York when the decision was taken?"

"Yes."

"In the theatre?"

"No, I was staying with friends. I rang the box-office on Monday morning and they broke the news."

"Would you give us the name and address of your friends, please." He looked surprised.

"Yes, of course." He dictated it to Mullin.

"They would be able to confirm that you were at their home and had made that call would they, sir?" Newton asked.

"No, actually, they wouldn't," Willie admitted. "Both of them work you see, the kids were at school. I was alone in the house."

"But there will be a record of that call and the one you made subsequently, to Ashley Fallowfield."

147

"Well, to be quite honest . . . I used the phone outside the village post office. I'd popped down there for some stamps."

"What about the second call, sir?"

"Same thing. It only takes five minutes to the village on one of their bikes. Ringing Fallowfield meant long distance, I didn't want to abuse their hospitality."

"So no record on either occasion?"

"Terribly sorry, Inspector." It was plausible but a shade too glib for Newton's liking. As was his custom, he changed the subject.

"You've already learned of your inheritance, I take it?"

"Rather!" Henderson chuckled, "I'm sure it was the last thing Margarite intended, but what a stroke of luck for us she hadn't made a new Will." Newton was even more aware of signs of carefully disguised poverty.

"Have you any idea how much . . . ?"

"Not yet. It's the house, mainly. I don't think the contents are worth anything. From what I remember, her income from investments would die with her because that's how Barker arranged it. As far as Mel and I are concerned though, anything's welcome. We'd invested too heavily in that play. I can't think why it failed, it was such a success in 1954." And Willie Henderson frowned, apparently more concerned with that disaster than providing himself with an alibi.

Newton moved on to the all-important question, "Where were you between twelve thirty and one thirty on Monday last, Mr Henderson?" Willie blinked.

"Is that when Margarite was . . . ?"

"Where were you, sir?"

"In York. Or rather, at my chums' place which is about ten miles due east."

"Why didn't you return straight away? Why stay on three more days if the play had been cancelled?" Henderson looked uncomfortable.

"Moral obligation of a sort. Singing for my supper, in fact."

"I beg your pardon?"

"The chums had been planning to bring a party of their friends to the theatre on Monday night. I'd promised to be the guest at a supper afterwards. Tell a few jokes, that kind of thing. It was a 'do', to raise money for the church or some such."

"So you stayed on?"

"I didn't want to let them down."

"Why not return on Tuesday?"

"Quite frankly, I was ill. After those Sunday papers I needed to get smashed. On Monday night everyone kept saying, 'What a pity about the reviews,' etc, etc. The chums knew I'd once been married to Margarite, of course, but they kept schtum about that. To be honest, I wasn't concerned about the murder, after the way Margarite behaved . . ." he hesitated then recovered. "I was far more bothered about what effect those disastrous notices would have on my career. The booze was flowing freely so I over-indulged. If the phone rang on Tuesday morning, I never heard it. I didn't surface until tea-time."

"And yesterday?"

"Ah well, Gemma — she's their youngest — was in the school play. Again, it was a courtesy thing to go and see it but I'd nothing better to do. It wasn't likely there'd be any casting directors hollering for my services after critics had labelled me 'yesterday's man'. I decided to lie doggo for one more day and return this morning as originally planned."

"When did you contact Miss Pelouse's solicitor, sir?" asked Mullin.

"Er, yesterday, about two thirty. After Mel had given me the message."

"Did you call him from the village box?"

"No, I used my chums' phone this time. When I told them what Mel had said, that the chap wanted me to contact him urgently, they urged me to do so."

"But you waited until the afternoon?"

"Cheap rate starts after lunch," Willie replied promptly. "I'm used to watching the pennies. Besides, I'd no reason to suppose it was good news. I thought the bit . . . Margarite — had probably left instructions for me to pay for her bloody funeral, that was far more likely. Ours was not an amicable parting, Inspector."

"The bequest came as something of a shock in fact?"

"Good lord, yes!" He sounded utterly sincere, "I was bowled over. I yelled my head off. Ask my friends, they'll tell you. And then I rang Mel, of course."

"During that conversation, Mrs Henderson didn't mention our intended visit?"

"No she didn't. I must have phoned her before you did, Inspector."

It was all pat and Newton distrusted it. "Returning to Monday morning, sir. If the production had not been cancelled, what would you have been doing? Rehearsing?" There was an infinitesimal pause.

"Possibly. The director was keen if he thought something needed polishing."

"Isn't that how a play gets knocked into shape before opening in London?"

"Yes, but this was an established piece so there was no re-writing — the usual reason for extra rehearsals. Between you and me, it's a damn fine play. Perhaps a little too sophisticated for a provincial audience." Newton nodded in apparent sympathy.

"Understudy rehearsals, Mr Henderson. Were any of those scheduled?" Willie laughed, a shade nervously.

"My word, you know the ins and outs of it, Inspector."

"Hardly, sir. But were the understudies due to rehearse that day?"

"They may have been," he replied carelessly. "Quite honestly, with all the hassle I can't quite remember what the original plans were."

"Perhaps your company manager would recall them, sir?"

"If it's that important?" There was an edge to his voice which Newton chose to ignore.

"I'd simply like to establish what the original plans were, for the relevant period on Monday."

"You're not suggesting I travelled down from York, sneaked into the studios and stuck a knife in Margarite — that's too silly for words. I'd gone on tour to try and re-establish myself as an actor, Inspector. I'm sick and tired of being told my face doesn't fit any more. Ask my agent, he knew how I felt. Last Sunday's papers were a monumental kick in the balls. It'll be years before

I'm offered another part — but I didn't kill Margarite! Dammit, I didn't even know about the Will until yesterday afternoon!"

"Thank you for being so frank, Mr Henderson." Newton was at his most mild. He rose, "We'll leave you to recover from what must have been a traumatic week." Willie Henderson glanced at him, suspecting sarcasm. "Tomorrow, I shall require you to come to the station and make a full statement giving complete details of your movements since last Friday."

"Yes, rather." It was the standard line in so many parts, but today Willie was unconvincing.

"If you could recall a witness for any of the events on Monday morning, we would be grateful for a name and address."

"Understood." He hugged his wife as if for support. "There must have been someone, Mel," he pleaded, but she couldn't help. Newton made a move. "Here, let me show you out." He led them the short distance into the hall. "What happens if I can't think of anyone?" he asked shakily. "Once you're branded a failure, people avoid you, Inspector. Last Monday morning, I was a leper. On Tuesday I nursed a hangover on my own."

"Sleep on it," Newton advised. "I'm sure something will occur to you."

The door closed and their footsteps receded. Willie turned to his wife. "For God's sake, Mel, what am I going to do?"

"Letting him off lightly, weren't you?" Mullin grumbled. "According to you, he was the only one with a motive."

"The only one we know of," Newton corrected. "It's tantalizing . . . The closer we get, the further we seem to be from the truth."

"*Was* that the truth?"

"Some of it, I think. I'm as uneasy as you are about the rest."

"They'd lost their savings, they must have been desperate."

"But the production was only cancelled on Monday morning."

"It must have been *discussed* after the other backers had seen the reviews. I bet Henderson knew then the play wasn't going to continue."

"Possibly . . . but think what a lucky coincidence it would have been to find Margarite Pelouse on her own in that tent — apart from knowing where to lay his hands on a surgical knife."

Newton kept to himself the knowledge that if Monday had been designated for understudy rehearsals, this would have left Henderson free until the half-hour call, at five to seven that evening. And wasn't York now part of the London commuter belt because of a two and a half hour train journey? He pushed both facts to the back of his mind.

"We're dealing with an actor," he pointed out. "A has-been but with a well-known face. Willie Henderson couldn't wander unrecognized among TV people, everyone at Rainbow would have known who he was."

"It *could've* been a classy bit of acting, in make-up and a disguise."

"He's not that good an actor," Newton said disparagingly, "he's the sort who always plays himself. Besides, as we've already agreed, security at Rainbow is tight. Even unrecognized, Henderson couldn't have got past Reception." Newton closed his eyes to the possibility of the fire escape because it smacked of incredibly good planning. From what he'd just seen, he didn't believe the Hendersons capable.

"I suppose Pelouse wasn't trying to entice him back?" Mullin suggested half-heartedly. "She was bored with Cornish — maybe she knew Henderson was short of cash and tried to lure him by telling him about the Will?"

"Can you imagine her doing so?"

"Not really," Mullin admitted. "The solicitor swore Henderson had no prior knowledge of the contents and she sounded too mean to offer money unless it was to entice a new boyfriend." That triggered something in Frank Newton's memory, but he couldn't put his finger on it.

"If only Henderson will come clean. He was being evasive, which worries me, but it's probably something trivial like a parking offence rather than a murder. Oh, why the hell can't one person have a convincing, hundred per cent bullet-proof alibi for NOT killing Margarite Pelouse!" Newton's irritation increased. "We'll probably discover half the crew had valid reasons for wanting to stab her as well."

"I still think we should pull Walsh in."

"Why exactly does he get up your nose, Sergeant?"

They negotiated the next roundabout before Mullin said sulkily, "He reckons some women watch the television because they fancy actors more than their husbands."

"Which they undoubtedly do."

"Including my wife." There's no answer to that, thought Newton. Nevertheless he wanted to squash stupid prejudice.

"Sexy acting doesn't make a man a murderer, Sergeant."

Taxi travelling through Kilburn

It had been "an experience", that was the only way Mr Pringle could bring himself to think of it. His shy soul had curled up into a tight little ball at times yet he had to admit, it had been a wonderful, gloriously entertaining afternoon. And Mrs Bignell had enjoyed herself, no doubt about that.

Sprawled expansively, she sat beside him full of champagne, bonhomie and a reckless bravado concerning her tight red shoes. "I do not care if I never get my feet into them again," she sighed, "I should never have bought them in the first place. I fell in love with the colour, that's all it was." Mr Pringle recognized a need for tact.

"I'm not surprised. They're very pretty and they match your dress." Mavis viewed the vivid pink and red roses complacently.

"They do, don't they," and feeling a need to explain, "that's why I bought them."

"Yes . . ." The taxi swerved and both shoes rolled across the floor. "I'm afraid they may get dirty down there."

"Put them in your pocket then," she urged. "I shan't be able to get my feet into them again today, not after all that dancing. Isn't Ashley a lovely boy!"

Mr Pringle was forced to recall certain aspects of the afternoon.

"It was — a most spectacular tea party. You and he performed quite a cabaret. I had difficulty remembering you had not danced together before."

"He's a natural," Mrs Bignell assured him. "When someone

153

like that takes hold of you, it's wonderful. You just float away . . ." She let go the strap and slid across the leather seat. Mr Pringle put an arm out and when Mavis found his cheek unexpectedly close, she gave it a warm, lingering squelchy kiss. "It never happened like that with Herbert." Mr Pringle was silent out of embarrassment as well as in tribute to the late H T Bignell. "You didn't mind," Mavis said gratefully. "You just sat and watched."

"I like seeing you dance," he insisted valiantly. "Champagne has a certain effect, I've noticed before. The sparkle transfers itself from the wineglass into your eyes, or rather your feet on this occasion. As you know, I am a follower of Minerva rather than Terpsichore —"

"You didn't mind, not even when we did the *paso doble*?"

"I've never seen it performed on a table top before."

"We did take the cloth off," she reminded him. "Ashley used it as his cloak, just like Torvill and Dean." There was a pause and he wondered uneasily what was coming next. "Do you think Ashley's a little bit, you know . . . Gay?" Mr Pringle thought of the extravagant posturing, the tightly waisted suit and pretty curls but he felt tenderly protective towards Mavis.

"A little bit perhaps. I shouldn't let it bother you."

"Weren't those Americans lovely? I thought they'd never stop cheering — and those waiters!" The taxi began to slow down.

"I think we're almost there. Mavis, are you sure it's wise to go barefoot? The pavements nowadays . . ." but she was calling to the driver.

"Has your wife got small feet, dear?"

"I've no idea, missus. They're always cold when I get into bed, I know that."

"Here." She pushed the shoes into his lap. "Give her these. An' take her dancing, that'll warm her up." The man was still grinning when he demanded six pounds fifty from Mr Pringle.

Mavis Bignell passed unscathed over broken glass and turds. She climbed the crumbling stone steps but was brought up short by the entry panel. ". . . twenty three, twenty four doorbells."

154

She stepped backwards to stare up at the shabby frontage. Mr Pringle moved quickly to prevent her tumbling into the area below.

"Where do they all live? There can't be that many rooms."

"I imagine the property is subdivided . . . Bowman 18F," he read and pushed at the front door. It wasn't locked. "I fear there may not be a lift."

The stairs were filthy. Feeble bulbs stayed alight only seconds, but what they revealed on each half-landing made Mr Pringle queasy. Mavis became increasingly indignant and he was aware of hostile, listening ears. Behind one of these doors was sure to be a man much larger than himself.

"What a pong! Doesn't anyone ever clean in here?"

"I doubt if there's a caretaker —"

"All this rubbish could attract vermin. Rats."

"Possibly the warmer weather may have contributed — Aah!"

But it was only a cat who spat and sped away because he'd trodden on her tail.

"Keep going," Mavis said heartlessly, "I think it must be one of the attics."

At this level the bulb was broken. Mr Pringle fumbled with the key. Inside the room was darker still and he pressed the switch.

"Fffph!" Mavis fanned with her handbag vigorously. "Don't they believe in fresh air?" He moved across, stooping to avoid the sloping ceiling and pulled back the curtains. There was only half a window because the room was bisected by a false wall and the single pane let in a paltry amount of daylight.

"How dreadful to live here," she said, quietened by what she saw. "The poor old thing."

It was a place of transit in a downward spiral of living, containing the minimum of furniture, with stained, dirty walls. Mr Pringle struggled to open the half-window and inhaled a wisp of oxygen gratefully. As he did so, the overhead light went out.

"Everything's on a meter," Mavis said in disgust. "When you're this far down, you spend your life putting coins in a slot. If you've got any."

Floor space was limited. Mr Pringle flicked a handkerchief

155

over a chair and she sat, gazing at the ancient, sticky patches embedded in the cheap carpet. "I wish I'd kept my shoes now."

"We'll buy you another pair."

"Not round here, dear. They won't have my sort." She examined the room, item by item. "This is all he had then. No home, hardly any clothes . . . He was careful though." Mr Pringle saw through the half-open wardrobe door well-pressed garments with tissue padding the wire hangers, presumably because employment depended on a smart appearance. Shoes too had been stuffed with newspaper to keep their shape.

"I gather from Fallowfield that Bowman had had a drink problem which once led to a brush with the law. He lost his licence and went to prison for several months. When he came out, he found it impossible to obtain work."

"It must've been serious?"

"Fallowfield didn't say. When Bowman finally contacted Rainbow, they offered employment on condition he stay sober."

Mr Pringle moved cautiously to the bed. "I imagine the blankets will be here." On top of the bedspread was a large envelope with an official stamp. "The police have returned his belongings."

"Poor old thing," Mavis repeated with a sigh. "Fancy ending up here. What a life!"

The envelope had been ripped open, presumably by another tenant, and when Mr Pringle picked it up, the familiar carrier bag fell out, spilling its contents. He put these on the table. Mavis examined the face on a bus pass.

"Mr Bowman was nice-looking then?" Mr Pringle remembered the elegant head.

"I believe he was, yes."

"Is this him when he was a young man?" She'd found a photograph album among a pile of books on the sill. "It can't be, it's more like Jack Buchanan." She read the inscription aloud, "'Sincerely yours, G S Beaumont'. That's what film stars used to put, 'Sincerely yours'. Perhaps this was an actor your chap worked with in the old days."

"Mavis, are these the blankets, d'you think?" Mr Pringle was searching among the bedding.

"Did you say he'd given up drink?" She'd picked up the small hip flask among the items on the table, "I noticed this the other day among his things. Nice, isn't it." She unscrewed the top, sniffed and said in surprise, "He must've been on the wagon there's only water in here. I wonder why he bothered to carry it about?" Mr Pringle took it from her.

"Water? The leather looks expensive. The flask could be crystal."

"Probably why he kept it on him. With the sort of neighbours he'd got here, someone would've pinched it." She found another item, "Is this a photo of his girlfriend?"

"I've no idea. Could you help me remake the bed?"

"Oh no, it's got 'Rainbow Property Store' on the back." Mr Pringle gave up bed-making.

"So it has. Perhaps we'd better return it, it obviously doesn't belong here. Are you quite sure there's only water in this flask?"

"I am a barmaid, dear."

"Everyone spoke as though Bowman must be inebriated and therefore partly responsible for the accident, although it didn't appear so to me."

"Why not tell the police what we've found? If he wasn't drunk they ought to know before the inquest."

"Yes . . ." Mr Pringle fingered the photograph absently. "This looks as if it belonged in a frame. One of the property photographs had gone missing according to Alix."

"Perhaps he found it and didn't know who to hand it to." Mavis returned to the photo album. "He must've worked a lot with this G S Beaumont — d'you think he might've been his stand-in? They used to use them in films." She stopped flicking the pages, "I wonder if *this* one was his girlfriend? It's got . . . 'An meinen lieben Man, von seinem lieben Frauchen', whatever that means?"

Mavis frowned, then she said, "Let me have that other one again, dear, the Rainbow photograph." She put the two side by side. "D'you know, I think this is the same girl. She's wearing an old-fashioned dress in the Rainbow photo but she's got the same look about her, hasn't she? Full of vitality. I wonder who she was?"

Mr Pringle took the two over to the daylight to compare.

"I think I'm beginning to guess," he said slowly.

"You don't have to — there's a signature underneath that bit of German." But it wasn't the name he'd been expecting.

There was one last surprise when they came to remake the bed. Mavis spotted the line of stitching along the edge of the mattress. "It's what people always used to do when they wanted to hide something." Mr Pringle protested but only weakly. With his penknife she slit the threads and withdrew from between the smelly wadding a post office savings book.

"This should be handed in to the police." He was glad to have a positive reason to go to them, he wanted to clear up his theory concerning the photographs. "Mavis, I don't think you should pry further —"

"A thousand pounds! I thought Mr Bowman was supposed to be broke?"

"Let me see." But she continued to peer at the franking mark.

"Deposited on Monday in a W1 post office. Before that, he'd only got seven pounds forty three pence."

Mr Pringle took the book and when he'd finished staring at it, looked at her, greatly troubled. "I don't understand."

"What about?"

"None of it makes any sense."

"You tell the police, dear. Let them have the worry, it's what they're paid for."

Mr Pringle used the same plastic carrier bag to remove various items and left a receipted list of what he'd taken, because his orderly nature required it.

"Good idea," Mavis approved. "You leave that where the other tenants can see. If they know you've got the bank book, it might stop them wrecking the room."

Outside The Bricklayers, he bade her farewell, promising to return at closing time. Once in his own home, Mr Pringle made himself a pot of tea and retreated upstairs to his study with the tray.

He sat until daylight faded, gazing alternately at the pictures on the walls and the items on the desk. Once, because it distracted him, he put the savings book aside and concentrated instead on the crystal flask and the two photographs. He remembered that Bowman had owed Alix money and added another note to his list. Surely the police could arrange for her to be recompensed from the thousand-pound deposit?

After the excitement of the Ritz, he felt tired. Thoughts were nagging away and until these were resolved, he knew he wouldn't sleep. Moreover he needed a clear head before he went to the police station in the morning. He stood by the window and gazed unseeing at commuters hurrying by in the dusk.

On their way home in the taxi Mavis had said, "Mr Bowman must've been a real gentleman, taking the blame for the accident and not wanting the driver to suffer."

"If that's what he meant . . ." Mr Pringle murmured to himself. Gradually, a possible solution to the puzzle began to emerge and like the names on the photographs, it wasn't what he'd expected.

Police station. Incident room

Walking toward the incident room, Frank Newton was in high good humour. A couple of hours spent with the hitherto reluctant landlady and the tube train death was moving toward a satisfactory conclusion. They hadn't let her go yet. It was late afternoon. Another half-hour and she'd begin fretting about her children returning from school to an empty house — he'd known women become extremely co-operative under those circumstances.

He felt a prick of irritation at seeing a group round one of the desks. Blaney had obviously come back with a tale. Someone spotted him and their laughter subsided. Newton forced himself to sound genial.

"Anyone find a murderer among the crew?"

"Sorry, sir. One conviction for driving under the influence, one larceny and Blaney unearthed a bigamist all by himself."

"Oh, well done." Blaney blushed.

"I found one of the addresses I'd been given didn't match the phone number."

"Who are we talking about?"

159

"An engineer, Laurence Geoffrey Wood. Tiny bloke. Forty-seven — you wouldn't think he'd have the energy."

Whoops! thought Sylvia Mackenzie.

"So I went to the address . . ." Blaney launched into his story once more. "The woman there — she's in her late forties as well — says she's Mrs Wood. Her hubby, Larry, was out. She says he's doing an outside broadcast somewhere in the Midlands and she's not expecting him home for a couple of days. I happen to know Wood was at the studios because I saw him there this morning. I didn't say anything but as I was leaving, I asked if I could use the phone. She shows me the one in the hall. Different number, different code altogether. I didn't let on. I rang the other number as soon as I found a call box. The second woman says *she's* Mrs Wood." DPC Blaney looked sheepish. "I thought I'd better check."

"You wanted to see his bit on the side, go on admit it, Blaney."

Amid the laughter, Newton asked, "And?"

"She says she's his wife as well, sir. Three young children this time, one still in the pram. She calls him Geoff and says he's on irregular shifts."

"One way of describing it —"

"I made discreet inquiries," Blaney said primly. "It all checked out. If he's not with one, he's definitely with the other."

"Apart from stretching his resources," Newton commented, "was there anything to connect Wood with the Pelouse inquiry?"

"Nothing," Blaney sighed, "but it was an interesting morning's work."

"What about the cameraman?"

"Ah . . . Mr Simon Lindsey. He's definitely only got one wife — and she knows he's been two-timing her. At least, that's the impression I got. They were both at home when I called."

"Anything relevant?"

"It was extremely difficult getting Lindsey on his own. The wife kept sticking her head round the door and demanding to be told. Lindsey was anxious to spill the beans but without her overhearing. Apparently she's been threatening divorce, which is the last thing he wants. Lindsey also claimed Jacinta Charles 'threw herself at him', although my impression was that *he's* the one who thinks he's irresistible. He made sure I knew there'd been others — in a whisper. He admitted to the quarrel under the boom and said that was because he was trying to break it off with Miss Charles. Afterwards, he handed over to his tracker and went up to the camera office."

"Why?"

"He said he had to check his roster for the following week and the camera office secretary confirmed this, but claimed the real reason was that Lindsey kept nipping up there to phone his wife. Ever since she got wind of the affair with Miss Charles, Mrs Lindsey's been making a nuisance of herself. The secretary was fed up with it. If Lindsey doesn't phone home at regular intervals, Mrs L is on the line like a shot."

"With justification," Doreen Dexter interjected.

"Whatever, it gave Simon Lindsey an alibi. I asked Mrs Lindsey if they'd had a long conversation on Monday. In between yelling that Simon was a randy bastard, Mrs Lindsey managed to tell me that the BBC news had been on at the time. That runs from one to one thirty. I got the impression they weren't in collusion on the matter, sir."

"Doesn't sound like it," Newton agreed.

"Which brings us back to Walsh," said Mullin.

Regular members of the team were aware of Newton's reluctance. He had a crablike approach to an obvious target — he needed to satisfy himself that nothing else had been overlooked before bringing Walsh in again. They knew he must be finding Mullin's brash approach offensive. No one spoke. Both DPWs avoided Newton's gaze as he waited for their opinions. Blaney, while agreeing that it had to be Walsh, held his tongue. Wicander appeared to be examining paperwork in one of the files.

"Any other information?" Newton asked, procrastinating.

"A message from the dresser, Henry Titmouse," Edwards, the Receiver said promptly. "He's on his way here."

"What's it about, any idea?"

"It's good and bad news, sir. The woman who washes the costumes on Thursday mornings found a pair of overall trousers with blood-stains on them. Unfortunately for Forensic, she put them in with the rest of the washing before telling Titmouse."

"Shit! What sort of overall trousers?"

"That's the bad bit. Operating theatre staff including anaesthetists all wear the same because of budget restrictions. According to Titmouse, this particular pair could have been worn by almost anyone. Five pairs had been issued on Monday but they're baggy garments, not sized. He didn't know who'd worn this particular pair."

"What about the stains?" This time Sylvia Mackenzie answered, reluctantly.

"The laundry woman uses biological powder because Rita Phelps insists on it." Newton groaned. "Henry wrapped the trousers in plastic straight away apparently, but I doubt if there's much left for Forensic."

"I want Henry Titmouse questioned very thoroughly indeed," Newton insisted. "If necessary, take him back to the studio and stand over him while he goes through each and every costume and tells you who wore what."

"Right."

"And make sure that wretched Phelps woman is somewhere else otherwise our Henry gets flustered." Mackenzie nodded. "As for Ian Walsh, we'll bring him in for a chat once Willie Henderson has made his statement."

Newton summarized the interview with the Hendersons, emphasizing the unease he and Mullin had felt. "It's best if we let them stew for a while. Make an appointment for ten a.m. Sergeant, and lay it on a bit heavily. If they're nervous they might talk."

"Understood, Guv."

"After Henderson has made his statement — if he can prove he's in the clear — that's when we'll pull Walsh in." He glanced at his watch. "D'you think our landlady friend will be anxious for another chat by now?"

The meeting broke up, but DPW Dexter came after him with a phone message. "That was Forensic confirming the Bowman hit and run car. Flakes of cellulose match those found on his clothing."

"Fine."

"They're trying to contact one of the men who has the use of the car. He's a part-time employee with the garage, perfectly satisfactory and a good driver but the thinking is he might have loaned the keys to a friend. The garage don't have an address for him, only a phone number."

"It shouldn't take long to wrap it up. Keep me informed."

"Yes, sir."

Mr Pringle's study

It was nearly dark when the doorbell rang and Mr Pringle wasn't expecting callers. When he opened the front door, the sight of a gnome baffled him. A wrinkled face stared up from beneath a matted, woolly cap, "Got a problem with the roof?"

"What — oh, yes. Yes indeed. Come in." Mr Pringle tried in vain to recall the name but his visitor thrust out a paw.

"Clarrie."

"How d'you do? Pringle."

"Right you are, Mr Pringle. Let's take a look while we still can, eh?" Mr Pringle watched anxiously as the gnome unloaded an extending ladder from on top of an elderly roof rack.

"You're not going up, are you?" he asked feebly.

"Don't you worry." Clarrie handled the sections deftly. "There's enough light left to see what's what." He climbed swiftly and having no head for heights himself, Mr Pringle closed his eyes.

Against a rising moon, he opened them in time to see the outline of the woolly hat bob along the ridge tiles and sit astride the chimney flank, whistling snatches of melodies for which Mr Pringle knew the words. The man must be of a similar age — surely not? To watch him tripping about up there without a harness, it was a worrying thought. At one point, Clarrie disappeared altogether. Mr Pringle rushed through into the back garden, convinced he'd find a small heap of bones topped by a green bobble hat lying on the patio, but the small man had already scrambled back whence he'd come and shinned down the ladder. He reached the ground and announced, as Mr Pringle came puffing back round the side of the house, "They don't build 'em like these nowadays."

"No," Mr Pringle agreed sadly.

163

"When these were put up, a man could take a pride in his work. After it was finished, he'd take the wife out for a walk on a Sunday and tell her, 'I built that,' and she'd feel proud an' all." For the first time, Mr Pringle began to experience a burgeoning hope.

"Shall we continue our discussion over a beer?"

"After I've seen inside the loft. Never take a drop until I've finished for the day."

"Through here." Mr Pringle led the way upstairs.

The master tiler's repertoire continued overhead as Mr Pringle put his two best tankards plus a couple of cans on a tray. On second thoughts, he added a third. When his guest descended he suggested, "There's a gas fire in my study."

Clarrie removed his headgear in deference to the new surroundings and proceeded to inspect the precious art collection. Mr Pringle wondered if he should explain their history, but Clarrie viewed them from his own perspective.

"He knew his roofs, this geezer did. You only get that angle of slope in the north-west because of the weather." Full of approval, he came to rest opposite Mr Pringle and wiped his mouth delicately. "Did Mavis tell you it would have to be a cash job?"

Mr Pringle swallowed his conscience.

"She did."

"I'd like to declare it," Clarrie was frank, "but if I do those income tax swines deduct it off me pension." Mr Pringle's hand trembled. He bent to mop up the splash. "You've got one or two problems, I'll not pretend you haven't," Clarrie eased a denture with his tongue. "It'll have to be both sides if we're to make a proper job of it." Mr Pringle steeled himself as the verdict was pronounced: "Couldn't do it for less than twelve hundred quid, I'm afraid."

The lowest quote so far had been five thousand pounds.

"Twelve hundred each side, you mean? Two thousand four hundred in all?" Clarrie looked pained.

"No, I do not. Twelve hundred the lot, provided we use what we can save of the old tiles." Mr Pringle was light-headed.

"Aren't they worn out? I thought everything had to be

stripped down to the rafters and thrown away?" Clarrie tore the tab off the second can with considerable contempt.

"What cowboy told you that? Your timbers is all right — and they don't make tiles that quality nowadays." Mr Pringle moistened dry lips, terrified this apparition sent by heaven would disappear, woolly hat and all.

"How soon can you start?"

The Newtons' living-room
Frank Newton struggled doggedly in an effort to finish *The Way of the World* because it wasn't in his nature to give in. As Jean put his night-time tea in front of him, Frank Newton closed the book with relief. "That's it, then. They all lived happily ever after."

"I doubt it," she laughed, half-serious. "I bet Millament and Mirabell fought like cat and dog on occasion. You didn't enjoy it."

"If you'd been in it and I'd seen it on stage, I might." She ignored the compliment.

"You remember I said I wanted to go back to work." He waited. "I've decided not to try acting again. That's over. Besides . . . I never really was good enough."

"Of course, you were!" But the protest was half-hearted and they both knew it. He waited nervously for an explosion.

Instead, Jean asked, "Did you mean it about someone to look after Emma? It would only be for a few hours a week but part-time work would give me a feeling of independence."

"Of course we can afford someone."

"I couldn't stand an office, or being behind a counter."

"No," he said carefully, "neither of those would suit you, I agree. Have you thought of anything else?"

"There's an advert in the High Street florists, they don't have a counter. It's mornings only, fifteen hours a week. I like working in the garden. Whenever I get het up, weeding or tidying the beds always calms me down. It might suit."

"You'd find an outlet for your artistic talents, too," he said prosaically, "working with flowers."

"I don't suppose they'd want me for that!" she scoffed. "They probably only need a school-leaver to sweep the floor and water the plants."

165

"People go to a florist when they need wreaths. I think you'd be very sympathetic in that situation."

"Mmm."

"Give it a try, Jean. You can always change your mind. Have you thought of anyone for Emma?"

She mentioned a neighbour with children of her own. His policeman's mind immediately assessed the pros and cons: a chaotic house with two boisterous boys but the woman was sensible when it came to childhood accidents. Jean read his thoughts.

"Laura is reliable."

"It's Emma, though. She's so used to being the only one." Immediately there was a shadow in her eyes and Newton could've kicked himself. It still hurt to be reminded of the two miscarriages. In the doctor's opinion these were the cause of the volatile behaviour, but when Frank suggested they try again, Jean refused. He guessed it was because she couldn't contemplate another failure and had been forced to hide his own disappointment.

"It'll probably do Emma good to have a bit of rough and tumble," he said boldly. If it meant sacrificing his daughter's timidity in exchange for Jean's happiness, then Emma must learn to cope. "You'd be back by the time she came home from school?"

"Laura would give her lunch with the boys and I'd collect her on my way home. That way she'd never be left alone."

"Fair enough. I'll pay. You settle the finances with Laura but keep your wages for yourself." Jean grinned.

"And I didn't even have to twist your arm. I might not get the job, of course."

"I expect you will, if you've set your heart on it."

On the way up to bed she asked, "How's the Pelouse case?"

"We're nearly there, I think. We're whittling the possibilities down, anyway."

"I hope what I said — about her being difficult — didn't influence you in any way?" Oh my dear girl! he thought. He kissed her gently.

"No love, it didn't."

166

10

A SECOND OPINION

Incident room. Friday morning
At ten a.m. Newton, Wicander and Edwards were studying the
enlarged studio floor plan. It was thickly covered with colour-
coded flags now, each cross-referenced and the office manager
was smug. "We've accounted for everyone. Most statements
have been corroborated at least twice. No unknown waifs or
strays."

"Show me Walsh's movement track." The pencilled line led
from the flag with his name, up as far as the closed ICU set door
before doubling back and exiting the studio via the wardrobe
room.

"It's based on his statement and confirmed by this chap here,"
the manager pointed to another flag, "the tracker on camera two.
He says Walsh went past while he was lining up a shot, hesitated
then turned back toward the wardrobe room. No way could he
have slipped unnoticed on to the set. Detective Sergeant Mullin
wasn't particularly pleased when he heard that this morning. He
seemed to have set his heart on it being Walsh." Frank Newton
didn't disagree.

"Who do the blue flags represent?"

"Extras. Their movement tracks are pencilled in in blue.
Yellow for actors, pink for members of the crew, green for other
staff, security men, cleaners and suchlike." Newton nodded
gloomily; the system was thorough even if it hadn't produced a
result. "You see how the extras' tracks converge on the
wardrobe room? Most went in there as soon as they'd finished
the corridor scene. The proper actors and actresses went upstairs
via this door here, to their dressing rooms —"

"Excuse me, sir."

"Yes?"

"Mr and Mrs Henderson have arrived. We've put them in number two interview room."

"Give them coffee and tell Mullin to join me down there in five minutes." Newton turned back to the diagram. "Which flag is Rita Phelps?"

"This one." The pink track meandered. "She couldn't make up her mind which direction she took when she left for a pee and the dressers contradicted themselves about it. Naturally, she swears she didn't go near the ICU set."

"Naturally."

The office manager sighed. "It's probably true. No one saw her head off that way and if she did go to the loo, it was in the opposite direction." He indicated the nearest lavatory.

"Which doesn't get us any further forward."

"We've *eliminated* a lot of the possibilities," Wicander protested. "We should complete the whole tally soon. At the studios, they're editing the episodes together today. The PA is doing a bit of cross-checking for us, noting exactly where people were using her time-code."

Edwards joined in, nodding enthusiastically, "We've never had such accurate information before."

Which wasn't much use if they couldn't solve the damn puzzle. Despite his words to Jean last night, there was still no real solution, nothing that felt right. And if the camera tracker had given Walsh an alibi, no wonder Mullin was miffed. Did it mean Henderson really was back in the frame? Could an old ham disguise himself sufficiently to slip into a television studios undetected?

"What about the fire escape, can that door be opened from the outside?" Wicander moved across to check with the computer operators.

"Apparently not," he called.

So unless Willie Henderson had an accomplice . . . ?

"I'll be downstairs if anyone wants me," Newton told Edwards.

"OK."

Mullin was already waiting. "Mrs Henderson insists on making a statement as well. She claims she was involved."

"Blast! Sounds as if they've concocted another tale." He walked into the interview room followed by Mullin.

Police station. Entrance desk
It had been a busy morning and by the time it was Mr Pringle's turn, the desk sergeant was harrassed. He vaguely recognized the face but couldn't understand the request. "If you've already made a statement about the accident, sir, that's all that's required."

"Further information has come into my hands, Sergeant. It is imperative I hand it over to someone in authority."

"I'll see if CID —"

"Could I please speak to the same officer who interviewed me before? It would save time." There was a rapid consultation and the sergeant bade him to, "Wait over there, sir". Mr Pringle went without demur. Throughout his life he'd been sent to an obscure corner whilst other, pushier individuals were dealt with first. He was constantly amazed that there should be so many very important people, all of them exuding self-confidence as they shouldered the rest of the world aside in the race to reach — what, exactly? And did they really live in those densely packed, executive, en suite estates?

Mr Pringle fantasized further. Suppose he was the only Indian left in a world full of cowboys, in danger of becoming extinct? Could he apply to the EEC for a grant in acknowledgement of his status? He straightened his shoulders: the last of the unimportant men, he was unique. It must count for something.

A lifetime of being snubbed had inculcated certain habits. Today, he'd bought the *New Statesman* as well as the *Guardian*. Thus fortified, he could endure a delay of several hours.

"Mr — Pringle?" It was the same young detective who'd taken his previous statement. There was a flicker of recognition. "Have you remembered something?"

"I have *discovered* facts which I believe to be relevant."

"We'd better have a talk." They walked past several doors labelled OCCUPIED. At the end of the passage, the detective found an empty room. Mr Pringle transferred various items from his attaché case on to the table top.

"I came across these yesterday, in Mr Bertie Bowman's flatlet in Kilburn. Here are the keys." He saw the raised eyebrows. "You may remember I went there originally to retrieve property belonging to Rainbow Television. A witness accompanied me."

"I see. Well, Mr Pringle, as we're presumably not discussing larceny, you'd better tell me why you brought these things here."

Police station. Interview room two

Newton didn't know whether he felt relieved or angry. Melissa and Willie Henderson behaved like naughty children who, once they told nanny, knew everything would be put right.

"You do realize it is an offence to waste police time," he began and then decided, forget it. Willie was obviously penitent and as a professional actor he'd endured enough failure for one week, even if he had ended up with a fortune. Newton didn't begrudge him an alibi; it confirmed his first instinct that there had to be a simple explanation.

"I'm so sorry, Inspector," Melissa Henderson was saying. "It's all my fault." She reached out her hand and Willie clasped it lovingly.

"We shouldn't have lied but Mel was terrified," he said comfortably.

"As I understand it, you had been booked for a recording session last Monday morning, Mrs Henderson. You claim you walked into Rainbow Television in mistake for the recording studio which was two doors further along the street, is that right?"

"Yes. It was a new address, I'd never been there before and I was late. I simply rushed inside without checking because from the outside it *looked* like a studio — which it is of course, but not a sound recording studio."

"You were due to do a radio commercial?"

"A ten second voice-over. I was a cosy teapot."

"I beg your pardon?"

"There were two of us. I was the cosy teapot, the other actress was the sexy one. It was an advert for tea-bags." Newton's eyes were more mournful than ever.

"Very interesting. And when you walked into Rainbow Reception, you say you saw Margarite Pelouse."

170

"Standing near the lifts. We'd never met but I recognized her at once. I was petrified. I realized I must be in the wrong building. The security man was shouting at me but I didn't stop, I simply turned tail and ran. Outside I checked the number and found the other studio almost immediately. But what scared me to death when I heard she'd been killed was the thought that I'd been there! I could've been the last person to see Margarite alive!" Melissa's over-dramatic actress's eyes implored him to understand. As far as Newton was concerned, it was a fuss about nothing.

"But this was early on Monday morning, Mrs Henderson," he reminded her patiently. "Of course Miss Pelouse was alive when you saw her, she wasn't killed until much later."

"I didn't know!" she wailed. "The reports of the inquest didn't say what time she'd been killed. All I could think about was how much she'd hated me — I was too frightened to think straight. I begged Willie to lie to help me out."

"The only real fib was about the phone calls, Inspector. Mel called me immediately and told me what had happened. Later, when I saw the ITN newsflash, I rang Ashley Fallowfield but he didn't tell me anything relevant — like the time of the killing — because your chaps warned him not to."

"We thought it best to keep quiet about my having accidentally been anywhere near the studio," Melissa Henderson was tearfully winsome.

Newton asked wearily, "Are you prepared to make a true statement now?"

"Of course, we are!" Willie was indignant. "As soon as you mentioned Monday *lunchtime* yesterday, Mel guessed we were in the clear but I still stuck to the fibs because that's what we'd agreed."

Frank Newton didn't let irritation show, he simply excused himself and asked Mullin to carry on. The possibilities were being eliminated much more quickly and now he wanted a few moments solitude before deciding who to tackle next. Outside the interview room, he heard his name being called.

"Good morning, sir. Someone's come forward with evidence relevant to the Pelouse case."

"Oh, yes?"

"He was a witness to the hit and run and he's been working temporarily at Rainbow, a Mr Pringle."

"Uh-huh."

"He's got some photos. He's in number eight."

"Right. Bring us coffee, would you." Better get the nutters out of the way as well.

Mr Pringle was relieved. This tall, quiet, rather dour man not only remembered who he was, he obviously intended to listen to what he had to say. The younger one had been a bit too brisk.

As they shook hands, he said diffidently, "It may be nothing but figments of an over-active imagination, Inspector."

"If you have taken the trouble to come here, you obviously don't think so."

"After Mr Bowman's fatal accident, one of the Make-up ladies happened to remark that no one can alter their back view successfully."

"I agree."

"I think that truism also applies to a profile, provided there has been no surgical intervention, of course."

Mr Pringle pointed to the two photographs and explained that one had been removed from the album, the other found among items in the carrier bag. "They are, I believe, the same woman. The one with Rainbow's stamp on it is only a snapshot but the other must have been taken in a photographic studio. It was Mrs Bignell who noticed it was the same face."

"Who?" Mr Pringle explained again.

"When I examined the album photograph, I realized I'd seen the same bony profile on television recently, but by then the subject was a much older woman. There is a signature on the back of that picture, underneath the German phrase. It was not what I expected, I must confess."

He watched Newton compare both photographs and saw recognition in his eyes. "I think you agree as to who she is. Perhaps you also know why she should sign herself with a different name? After thinking about it, I now have a theory."

Frank Newton considered both photographs for a moment then looked across at him.

172

"We understand she had two baptismal names," he said quietly.

"Ah." It wasn't quite as he'd imagined, but Mr Pringle was satisfied. "I thought she had changed it for theatrical purposes."

"In a way . . . Her second husband was an impresario. He made her into a star. That was when she became Margarite Pelouse." Mr Pringle nodded.

"I'm afraid my knowledge of such matters is extremely limited," he confessed. "However, I do remember when it was the custom for film stars to invent glamorous names for themselves." DI Newton didn't comment. "I am right in thinking it is the same profile?" Mr Pringle's confidence began to falter. "The one I saw on the television news the night she was killed? That was taken when Miss Pelouse was in her sixties and in costume. The beaky nose and tilt of the chin were much more assured because she was famous but I believe I'm correct?"

"I believe you are. My congratulations, Mr Pringle."

Mr Pringle had come to the worst bit and swallowed. "As I said, the album containing the second photograph was in Mr Bowman's bedsitter. There were others of that same young girl together with a handsome young man, all taken about the same period in the late thirties or early forties. Also theatrical poses of the same man on his own signed, 'Sincerely yours, G S Beaumont'." Newton looked at him narrowly. Mr Pringle nodded.

"I considered removing the album, then I realized you would doubtless prefer your experts to examine it *in situ*. When they do, the fresh fingerprints on it are those of myself and Mrs Bignell."

"G S Beaumont?" Newton repeated slowly.

"I copied it down, to be certain." Frank Newton stared at the page in the pocket book.

"Mrs Bignell referred to Jack Buchanan when she saw the photographs. I remembered another actor, well known for his profile: Ivor Novello. I thought Mr Bowman had a fine actor's head that day in the street."

Newton brooded silently.

"I believe that first photograph, the snapshot, is the studio one that went missing from Alix Baxter's property cage," Mr Pringle said eventually.

"Possibly."

"She told me it was supposed to be of *Dr Watkins's* mother. Last night, I came up with a possible theory . . . although it may be nonsense."

"May I hear what that was?"

"I wondered if Ian Walsh had been asked to supply the photograph himself. It seemed possible that a conscientious stage-manager might ask an actor if she could borrow a family portrait to ensure a better likeness."

And a bitter young man might want to wreak vengeance on an old woman who'd made a fool of him, a private demonstration that she was old enough to be his mother, thought Newton.

"Leave it with me, Mr Pringle. I'll see the photograph is returned to Miss Baxter, in due course."

"I wonder why Miss Pelouse changed from Erika to Margarite? Erika sounds glamorous enough, surely?"

"Not to an English audience at that time."

"Ah!" Another part of the puzzle slipped into place. "Mrs Bignell said the clothes looked continental. Those short socks with a full skirt, German women often dressed like that before the war. And Miss Pelouse naturally wanted to be discreet about her origins."

"Undoubtedly."

"Strange how fashions in names change," said Mr Pringle thoughtfully. "Nowadays I doubt whether Archie Leach would bother to rechristen himself Cary Grant. *Beaumont* probably looked much more romantic than Bowman. As for Bertie, although a form of Albert, it was also used as a diminutive of Gilbert when I was at school."

Great-Uncle Gilbert!

Mr Pringle pointed to the flask. "It was that which decided me to come here today, however. Mr Bowman had been accused of being drunk and therefore in part responsible for the accident; that flask contains nothing but water. He is entitled to credit for overcoming a handicap."

"The autopsy would reveal the alcohol level in the blood, Mr Pringle, but thank you for bringing the matter to our attention. The inquest on Mr Bowman is scheduled for this afternoon."

"Of course! How stupid of me."

174

"Not at all . . . Only water, you say." Newton picked up the flask. "Nice workmanship."

"If you unfasten the leather strap, the two small cups are engraved with a set of initials."

Newton unclipped them. "G S B and E M B?"

Mr Pringle sighed. "Unless I'm mistaken, those cups are gold. I think it was kept as insurance against an emergency. This last item, however, was concealed in a mattress. I took the liberty of looking inside." He opened the blue plastic cover. Newton saw the amount of the last deposit and the franking stamp of the Berwick Street post office.

One thousand pounds paid in on Monday!

"I questioned Mr Fallowfield this morning. Extras are not called in for rehearsal, apparently. They are required only on recording days, but Bertie Bowman was used regularly. I assume he discovered last week that Miss Pelouse was joining the cast and managed to make contact in some way." Mr Pringle shook his head sadly. "It's only guesswork, of course, based on my thoughts of last night, but as there was obviously a connection between Miss Pelouse and Mr Bowman, I assume he begged her for financial assistance. His circumstances were extremely tragic and she was the only person in the cast who could afford to be generous."

Newton's mind was racing: it all added up yet it couldn't be true. No one who'd been in that corridor scene could possibly have been in the ICU area at the same time; the two sets were over fifty feet apart. He found he was still holding the savings book.

"If the cheque was made out to the post office — it could have been paid in by anyone." Was that what Cornish had been searching for? It was as good as cash.

"I doubt if Mr Bowman had a bank account," murmured Mr Pringle.

"No."

"My German is rusty, Inspector, but in that message on the back of the album photograph, the woman refers to herself as a 'wife'."

The two looked at one another with complete understanding. "There is also this." Newton frowned.

175

"A plastic carrier?"

"Mrs Bignell and I used it yesterday, for one of the blankets. It was in Mr Bowman's hand at the time of the accident. I'm afraid he may also have used it the previous day. Presumably whatever he wiped his hands on was hidden in there." Newton gazed at the brown-coloured stains.

"Another excellent piece of observation," he said drily.

"I almost wish I hadn't seen . . . his was such a sad end."

Newton looked at him steadily.

"Miss Margarite Pelouse was brutally stabbed to death, Mr Pringle."

But it couldn't have been Bowman, screamed his brain.

Mr Pringle read again the fragment of emotion captured on the back of the photograph. "They loved each other once, I think."

Newton couldn't bring himself to respond.

"Thank you for your assistance, sir. I shall require you to make a further statement. We know where to contact you?"

"Yes." Mr Pringle rose to go. The overhead light glinted on the two small cups and the sparkling crystal flask. "Perhaps he couldn't part with a last reminder of that love." Newton took a more prosaic view; as far as he was concerned it was evidence for the Crown. "The words I heard Mr Bowman say before he died: 'My fault . . .' I thought he was referring to the hit and run driver. Last night I decided otherwise, although I still do not understand why he killed Miss Pelouse."

Neither do I, thought Newton grimly, and what was worse, whichever way you looked at it, it was bloody impossible.

"Leave that with us, Mr Pringle. Good day to you."

When the young detective returned, Newton asked briefly, "What's the latest on Bowman?"

"Records have turned up a manslaughter drunk driving charge in '82. He did nine months and lost his licence. The victim was a Miss Anne Goodhill . . . same surname as the part-time driver the garage owner told us about. Shouldn't be long before we locate him and confirm."

Had another piece fallen into place? It would have to be checked of course, but Newton began to feel confident.

"When we do find him," the young detective said cheerfully, "it should just about wrap it up for us."

"Keep me informed."

"Will do."

Newton strode into the incident room. "Are the Hendersons still on the premises?"

"No, Guv."

"I want Willie brought back here. Also that extra woman . . . what was her name?" He snapped impatient fingers, "The pantomime dame with the purple eyelids —"

"Oh, Iris Fanshawe."

"That's her. And we'll need to speak to Jacinta Charles."

"What about Walsh?"

"Later. Call the bank. I want to know if a debit of a thousand pounds has gone through Pelouse's account this week. Oh, and pull in Jason Cornish while you're at it." Mullin sounded subdued at the workload.

"Your wife rang. She said it wasn't urgent."

"Thanks." Newton turned to Wicander and Edwards. "I want a complete rundown on Bertie Bowman's movements throughout Monday. Pull out everything from the rest of the statements, OK?" He pointed to the diagram of the studio floor. "Show me Bowman's track throughout the corridor scene and afterwards. And find out what Records have under either Bowman or Beaumont, initials G S or B S, apart from one drunk driving charge. Also, that dresser, Titmouse, we'll have him in. I want to know exactly when Bowman went through Wardrobe and if anyone saw him take off his anaesthetist's gown. My guess is he did so before he left the set. Underneath, porters wear the same basic uniform as the rest of the medical characters . . ."

"But how could an extra . . . ?" Wicander began.

"I know. They were all in the corridor scene and we saw Bowman with our own eyes — but I don't bloody care. Somehow, Bertie Bowman, alias G S Beaumont, who may have been Pelouse's first husband, stabbed her to death while fifty feet away from the ICU set and while acting as a porter. It's wrong but there it is. Now, let's get at it."

*

Jean's voice was anxious. "I haven't interrupted —"

"Nothing important," he insisted firmly. "What's up? Is it Emma?"

"She's fine. I've got the job, that's all. A three week trial beginning Monday — and it will mean working with flowers, not just sweeping the floor."

"Well done! See if you can fix a baby-sitter and we'll celebrate at that new Indian place."

"Thanks!"

Ian Walsh was debating whether to risk calling Jacinta when his own phone rang. For one wild moment he thought it might be her. Instead Newton's quiet tones enquired politely, "Just a couple of questions, Mr Walsh. I understand a Property photograph went missing from the studio on Monday. We've had one brought to our attention and I thought you might help us identify it." There was a fractional pause.

"Props are nothing to do with me, Inspector. Try Alix Baxter —"

"We thought you might prefer to keep the identity of the subject a secret, Mr Walsh. I am right in assuming you supplied the photograph originally?" Again the question hung in the air, but not for long.

"You're sure it's the same one?"

"I have it in front of me, sir. On the back there's the Rainbow TV stamp, but no doubt that's how they protect everything that comes into the studio. I don't suppose you were particularly concerned to have the photograph returned?" Ian Walsh suddenly sounded very tired.

"It was a stupid thing to do. When Alix asked, I thought, what the hell. No one spotted who it was and it served to remind me how stupid I'd been. I'd forgotten it was there — it was just another object on the set — but Margarite saw it during the technical run on Sunday afternoon. She was livid — that's when things began to get vicious between us. When I heard the photo had disappeared, I thought she must have asked Jason to steal it."

"No, Mr Walsh, it wasn't Mr Cornish who did that."

*

178

Iris Fanshawe was frightened. To leave her sister-in-law's semi-detached in a police car gave her a certain *cachet* but DPW Dexter was no longer friendly.

Detective Inspector Newton was much more forbidding as well. Before she could even catch her breath, he'd accused her of being a liar. Iris Fanshawe summoned every scrap of histrionic defiance but he leaned across the desk, dark eyes suddenly menacing.

"One more untruth and you'll be on a charge this time, Miss Fanshawe. Now answer my questions — and don't be tempted to have the vapours. On Monday lunchtime you went up to the extras' dressing rooms on your own."

"I — I —"

"You knew one of the male extras always carried a flask. You wanted a drink. You went into their room and helped yourself —"

"There was nothing in it, only water!" He leaned back as exasperation got the better of him.

"Why the hell couldn't you have told us that before!"

"I wanted to protect Mr Bowman. Why should I reveal the straits to which he'd been reduced? In the old days there would have been Armagnac in that flask!"

You stupid cow, thought Newton in disgust. His voice was cold.

"You were obviously unaware that Mr Bowman no longer touched alcohol."

"How ridiculous! I've never seen him without that flask —"

"After leaving prison, madam, it's my understanding he never touched drink again." Mention of prison stunned her.

"How dreadful . . . I'd no idea," Iris stuttered then rallied. "He was a former artiste. Why should he be judged a failure at the end?"

"A man isn't a failure because he doesn't drink!"

"A gentleman would never carry water in a hip flask. I wanted to protect Mr Bowman's character!" Iris cried affectedly. God give me patience! begged Newton.

"What happened after Bowman caught you red-handed?"

"It must have been the shock. I've never known Mr Bowman use such language — he said there'd been an accident —"

"Exactly how did he describe it?"

"Something about the floor manager shouting, but it was all mixed up with wild accusations against me for touching the flask. He was in a terrible state. I offered to buy him a drink as it was obvious he couldn't afford one. He followed me on to the fire escape, shouting insults. I felt I had to get away —"

"Which way did Mr Bowman go?"

"I don't know! Towards Oxford Street."

"And you?"

"My nerves were in a dreadful state —"

"Which pub was it? Come along, Miss Fanshawe, I want to know where, for how long, and how many drinks." Iris Fanshawe lost all desire to impress.

"The Grapes. The glasses are reasonably clean."

"Did Bowman have his carrier bag with him?"

"He always did. He thought he was less likely to be mugged with a tatty thing like that."

"Miss Fanshawe, I shall require you to make another statement. DPW Dexter here will assist you. If it's a pack of lies like the last one, you could end up in the cells." Iris's silly eyes were round with terror. "I also want you to show us on a street plan, the precise direction Mr Bowman took when you and he parted company."

The franking in the savings book was clear enough, but he wanted every scrap of evidence confirmed even if Bowman couldn't possibly be the killer.

As he rose and delivered a final, "Nothing but the truth, remember that," Iris Fanshawe imagined she could see a black cap in the aura above his head.

Willie Henderson sagged with anxiety. "What now? I thought we'd cleared everything up this morning?"

"It concerns another aspect of the case, sir. I wondered if you could tell us anything about Miss Pelouse's first husband?"

"Old G S? Sorry, no I can't. He'd disappeared off the scene years before I knew her. Don't think Alfred Barker ever knew much about him, either."

"What was his surname, sir, do you happen to know that?" Willie looked surprised.

"G S Beaumont. Margarite dropped a *few* words about him, occasionally. He was an English actor working in Germany when they met. Pre-war continental B movies. He never made it over here. My guess is he hadn't much talent. He used to play the archetypal Englishman, always pulling up his coat collar, tweaking his hat and fiddling with a cigarette." Willie chuckled, unaware he'd described his own role in a later decade, "Probably the Huns' idea of an English spy! Margarite admitted she'd only married him to get British nationality, but claimed he'd let her down. Old G S had boasted wealthy family connections, but when they landed, she discovered he'd been chucked out of the parental nest years before for daring to become an actor. The family refused even to see them." Willie grinned again. "There weren't many who managed to put one over on Margarite. I'm afraid old Gilbert paid the penalty. He couldn't get work and when she divorced him, he lost his meal ticket."

Newton paused before asking his next question. "Do you happen to know if Mr Beaumont was in love with his wife?" Willie stiffened.

"Why ask me a thing like that? She divorced him in order to marry Barker. She never got over being chucked out by *him*."

"It's not Miss Pelouse or Mr Barker but Mr Beaumont who interests me, sir." Willie shifted uneasily.

"God knows what happened to him . . . must be dead by now. He sounded an easy-going sort . . . she led him a bit of a dance. There were other chaps during their marriage, as there were during ours. Dear Margarite had a voracious appetite — Barker was the only one she really cared for, of course. And when she was young, she was very beautiful . . . as well as determined to get to the top." Newton waited because the question hadn't yet been answered. Eventually Willie said, "If the poor bastard felt as I did about her, he must have been besotted. Thank God I met Mel."

Newton was not prepared to waste time on Jason Cornish. "What do you know about the thousand pound cheque?" Jason flared briefly.

"Where did she hide —"

"How did you find out about it?"

"She was at the bureau filling in the stub when I walked in on Sunday night, that's how. She shoved it in her handbag and I never saw it after that. She said he'd repay every penny in the end."

"He?"

"Walsh of course. They'd had a spat in the rehearsal room. He must've demanded cash instead of an apology. He nipped into the tent when I went for coffees Monday morning. She was really worked up when I got back."

"Did she say anything else?"

"That nobody would succeed in humiliating her."

"Why didn't you tell us before?" Jason shrugged.

"Nothing to do with me . . . I knew what Walsh must've gone through . . . She deserved what she got, in my opinion."

Hendon. 5A Blake Road

The neighbour watched both policemen from behind her nets before venturing up to the fence. She waited until one of them had finished banging on the front door.

"He should be in."

The constable straightened up.

"Mr Goodhill?"

"That's right."

"When did you last see him?"

"Tuesday, I think," the neighbour said uncertainly. "Yesterday I *heard* him come home late. Heard the motorbike, then the garage door. Never saw him leave this morning. He doesn't always. It depends on whether he's got a job."

She watched the second policeman rattle the letter box and shout, "Mr Goodhill, are you there?"

"Keeps himself private. He's been ever so quiet lately."

"Yes."

"He used to be a church goer. C of E. We're Catholic." She waited, hoping they'd spot it for themselves, but when they failed to, she pointed it out. "His bedside light's still on."

"What?" They shielded their eyes against the glare of the setting sun. Without speaking, both came to the same conclusion and the woman guessed what it was.

"You don't have to smash the door down. He keeps a spare key under a brick in the shed."

"Christ!"

"It's all right," the older constable took charge. "You go downstairs and tell that busybody to make us tea. Say we'll be round in a few minutes — and don't let out what's happened."

"Shouldn't we — do something?"

"No point." The other man glanced round. "Where's the bloody phone?"

"I think I saw one in the hall." The white-faced constable swallowed. "Isn't there anything . . . ?"

"No, mate," but he felt a certain compunction. "Is this your first stiff?" There was a mute nod. The other reached out and checked the pulse. "Stone cold, like I said. Nothing we can do. We make a note of what we can see . . . the letter — that'll please the coroner — the girl's photo, etc. etc., but we don't *touch* anything. Now you get that tea organized and I'll make the call." He looked at his watch. "We discovered the body at seventeen thirty-five, right?"

"Yes."

Indian restaurant

It was early evening and the restaurant was comparatively empty. Frank Newton relaxed. Jean was happily excited for the first time in weeks and despite his problems, he shared her mood.

"I explained to Emma as soon as she got home from school," she told him. "She didn't seem to mind."

"What about Laura's two boys and their friends? Can she cope, d'you think?" Jean laughed.

"Don't worry. We went over together to tell Laura. Emma insisted on taking Matilda with her. She showed her to Ian and Keiran and laid into them — you should have heard her! She said she and Matilda would be visiting their house from now on and as this was her best dolly *no one* was allowed to touch Matilda without her permission — otherwise Daddy would be very cross!"

"I hope Daddy wasn't held up as some kind of threat?" Jean bubbled over.

"He *might* shout that they were bloody nuisances the way he did when Mr Barry's cat made a smell in the kitchen." Frank groaned.

"Out of the mouth of babes . . ." Jean raised her glass.

"To you, Daddy."

"And to you, my love."

"Hi!"

It was so unexpected, he choked. Pat beamed and thumped him on the back.

"You managed to hide yourself away!" She sat, uninvited, next to Jean who stared in bewilderment. "Hi, you must be Mrs Newton. I'm Pat, the PA."

"As a matter of interest, how did you know where to find me?" Newton gasped angrily.

"I asked that big chap with the small head."

"Detective Sergeant Mullin?" Pat had almost endeared herself to Newton, but not quite. "He had no business —"

"Oh, he didn't *want* to tell me. He was pretty useless, in fact. All he'd overheard you say was 'Indian restaurant' and there are five in this locality, that's what took me so long. Hang on a minute . . ." She rummaged in the vast leather sack that was a permanent fixture over one shoulder. A waiter appeared, hovering tentatively. "Oh, hi. Do you do take-away?"

"Yes, madam."

"Three vegetable curries and three poppadoms — and I'll have a lager while I wait." The waiter disappeared. "Damn! I forgot to ask if they'd got a VHS."

"What the hell for?"

Pat pulled out a video cassette. "It's all on here. I got the editor to copy it across and came straight here, via the incident room, of course."

"Copy what across, Miss Fagan?"

"Pat," she said patiently. "Nobody uses surnames in television."

"Would someone kindly tell me what is going on?"

Frank Newton cursed silently. The mood had evaporated and Jean was obviously as annoyed as he was.

"I'm sorry. This is Pat, from Rainbow Television."

"I'm the PA on *Doctors and Nurses*. Bernard and I have been editing the episodes today," Pat explained sociably. "On Monday, I knew there was something bothering me but I couldn't remember what it was. I promised your husband as soon as I remembered I'd come straight round and tell him. So here I am."

"Whilst I appreciate your keenness, Miss Fagan, surely the matter could have waited over the weekend?" Pat was miffed.

"No, it couldn't. It's desperately important." The waiter put the lager in front of her. "Oh, cheers! Have you got a video machine?"

"For the television . . . ?" The Bengali looked at her nervously. "In the kitchen . . . It belongs to the manager."

"Be a sweetie. Ask him if we can borrow it for five minutes." It was the self-confident assumption that all the world would give way to her wishes which irritated Newton most of all.

"Look, if you leave that cassette with me, I'll look at it later on this evening." Pat was adamant.

"I haven't signed for it and besides, I promised the editor I'd return it." She flashed her professional smile as the manager approached. "Hi, it's awfully kind of you. And I promise it won't take more than five minutes."

Angry though he was, Newton followed her through the baize door and was immediately engulfed in the spicy smells. Waiters and cooks stared as Pat, chattering ceaselessly, ejected one cassette and pushed home her own.

"This has got time-code all over it. It's the offline editing copy of the corridor scene —"

"I've already seen that!" But she shook her head.

"You've seen it, I agree. We all did. I stared at it till I was blue in the face, trying to remember. The trouble is what actually happened was so bloody obvious none of us noticed. Where's the gadget for this thing?" The manager handed it to her. "You have to compare both takes of the scene. Watch take one closely."

Despite himself, Newton leaned nearer the screen.

"Here's the VTR clock, and the time-code cross checks, this is take one . . . Three, two, one, zero — and there's the opening shot on two: a porter comes towards us pushing a body trolley. Cut to the wide shot . . . and that's where we freeze frame for a moment." Pat stopped the tape and looked at him expectantly. "What do you see?"

She spoke as if he were a five year old and she his nursery-school teacher.

"That porter pushing his trolley."

"Ignore him for a moment. He takes your eye because the cut between the two shots was on his action. Who do you see in the background?"

"Behind the other extras, the second porter beginning to go across."

Bertie Bowman alias G S Beaumont, establishing an alibi that couldn't be broken. He couldn't have stabbed his ex-wife fifty feet away in the ICU set. Newton's frustration was almost at bursting point. Pat however, looked so pleased with his reply, he wondered if she was about to present him with a bright red apple.

"What do you notice about that particular porter?"

"We know it's Bowman, Miss Fagan."

"That's the first important point, the one we all missed. Watch what happens next." She let the scene trickle forward. In slow motion the porter crashed once more into the wall. At the point of impact, Pat stopped the tape a second time. "That would never have happened if the right man had been pushing the trolley."

"What d'you mean?"

"It was *Bertie's* job to do things like that because he was a regular. That first extra had never done it before. Now watch take two."

Silently they saw the VTR clock disappear, replaced by the opening wide shot. As the cut happened and the porter rushed once more towards them, Jean Newton said in surprise,

"He's missing. The one going across the background, he's not there this time." Newton wanted to cheer, to hug this dreadful bossy girl and buy her champagne but instead, she spoke first and confused him.

186

"The sad thing is, we shall never know what he saw," Pat said, pressing the rewind button. Newton looked blank. "Bertie obviously didn't know we were doing a second take, he must have dashed off and been first in the wardrobe room. He probably saw whoever it was stuffing that gown in the dirty clothes basket."

Newton gathered himself together. He knew why she avoided looking at him.

"Very probably."

He helped her rewind the tape, paid for the curries and accompanied her to her car. All the while she was determinedly cheerful in front of Jean, he realized.

Once outside he said, "My wife is accustomed to hearing the murkier side of my work."

"You've no proof it was Bertie," Pat insisted valiantly. "I've asked the editor to make a copy of both these takes by the way."

"Thank you."

"He was such a nice old man . . . always courteous. I still can't believe — I mean, why? What possible connection . . . ?"

"Leave it with us, Miss Fagan." She managed to rub him up the wrong way one last time.

"At least I've stopped you arresting the wrong person. Ian and Jacinta might have been rotting in jail by now."

"We're not always wrong, you know."

"You can't tell me! I used to work on documentaries. Cheery bye. I suppose I should thank you for treating us to supper."

He watched her bump her old mini out of the tight parking place and returned to the restaurant.

"Was it him?" Jean asked.

"We think so."

"Why?"

"He was her first husband. He was desperate — she gave him money. I don't know what happened after that, whether she taunted him once too often. She was certainly in a position to be extremely cruel. She may have threatened to expose his past and his poverty to the Press — the poor old devil still had his pride. I think he still loved her too, which must've made it worse. I doubt if we'll ever know the whole of it." Jean shivered.

"How awful."

187

"Drink up. This is a celebration, remember. Here's to flowers." He reached over and kissed her cheek. "I hope they bring you peace, my love."

11

POST MORTEM

Studio A. Dr Watkins's bedsit. Ep. 51.

182   *Cam. 1*: (POS. B)
         TIGHT on hand pouring wine into glass
         TILT UP tO HIS FACE
         SEE his look at NURSE WILLIAMS

         CUT
183   *Cam. 3*: (POS. C)
         MID SHOT WILLIAMS
         SEE her look down

         CUT
184   *Cam. 1*: (POS. B)
         (WIDER) MS WATKINS
         PAN with him as he takes wine across

         CUT
185   *Cam. 3*: (POS. C)
         2-SHOT as WATKINS arrives
         SEE her look up as she takes glass

                    NURSE WILLIAMS: Thank you.

         CUT
186   *Cam 1.*: (Fast to POS. D)
         MID 2-SHOT. HOLD his kneel
         GO IN TO TIGHT 2S

                    DR WATKINS: Oh, my darling, you know
                    what this means . . .

         CUT
187   *Cam. 3*: (POS. C)
         BCU WILLIAMS O/S WATKINS

```
        FREEZE FRAME
        SUPER

188     Cam. 4:          END ROLLER.        SOUND: GRAMS.

        MIX
189     CAPTION      RAINBOW TELEVISION plc
                         © 1988
```

Ashley had had official confirmation from the Inland Revenue that his appeal had been dismissed. His financial adviser had managed to salvage something; the total sum for his mourning had been added to his single person's allowance for 1988/89, but that was all.

It wasn't in Ashley's nature to be down-hearted. The ratings for episode forty-one of *Doctors and Nurses*, transmitted with the tasteful addition of Chopin's 'Funeral March' dubbed over the badly framed shot of the body of Margarite, had had an accredited viewing figure of fifteen million. With that kind of track record, he could take his pick in the freelance world. "So many amateurs nowadays, thanks to Hilda," he murmured gratefully. "So many of them and so few of me — how can I fail?" It was the simple truth and already he'd put in an order for a Roller. Nothing flashy, just plain burnished gold. It would make the memory of Margarite infinitely precious.

He'd been at pains to point out to Rainbow's consortium that they couldn't pull that sort of trick every week, there weren't enough old actresses willing to be sacrificed but now, standing behind Bernard in the gallery, Ashley felt a glow as another heart-warming idea occurred to him.

"Jacinta's such good value. D'you think she and Ian will get back together?"

"They might," Pat clicked off her watch. "Thirty black. Quick spot check please, VTR."

"We'd get the front page of *TV Times* if they did."

"Clear on that last take, Pat."

"Thanks."

On the floor Robert shouted, "That's a wrap thank you, studio."

Newton's office a fortnight later

Newton read again the photostat of the camera tracker's statement and underlined one phrase in red:

"As I was getting in position to try out the shot, *an extra went past* and I noticed Ian Walsh . . ." In the margin Newton wrote, "Success in this job depends on attention to detail."

"I want this circulated this afternoon," he told his secretary, then stopped as Mullin appeared in the doorway. "Ah, you're off then, Sergeant? Back to Leicester?"

"Pity about the inquest." Newton didn't think so.

"What we expected. Waste of time to prosecute a corpse."

"He deserved to be," Mullin said doggedly. Newton didn't agree with that, either. Hadn't the poor bugger once been married to Margarite Pelouse?

"Yes, well . . . hope you feel you benefited from the experience. Safe journey."

Mr Pringle's study

The two figures on the sofa were loose-limbed in their contentment. Outside the wind howled and rain beat against the window panes. Mr Pringle listened to both with equanimity. "A dark and stormy night . . ." It was odd how his tongue found such difficulty with the words.

"No need to worry about that any more," said Clarrie. Mr Pringle nodded wisely as any owl.

"Noneedatall . . ."

"What d'you think of it?" Clarrie contemplated the sixth empty bottle in front of them.

"Bestofthelot . . ."

"I'm glad you think so . . . I reckon it's a good brew. Three of these'n I daren't go up a ladder." Mr Pringle decided he wouldn't either.

From the kitchen, succulent fragrances wafted upwards and curled about their nostrils making saliva run wild.

"I give this partic'la brew a name," Clarrie admitted proudly. "Dreadnought."

"Very-apposite . . . veryappositeindeed." Clarrie leaned back and listened to the downpour.

"That old roof'll see you out now, I reckon. Tight as a drum she is."

"Mmm."

"They don't build houses like this nowadays."

"No." Clarrie turned his attention to distant sounds in the kitchen.

"They don't make wimmin like that, neither. If you don't mind my saying so, Mavis is what I call — a proper sort. Well built in a different kind of way." A tear sprang to Mr Pringle's eye. He wanted to agree but was fast becoming incapable. When the call came to go below to supper, Clarrie took his arm. "I'll give you a hand."

The proper woman looked at them severely. "You're sozzled."

"Averylittlebit . . ." She waited until most of the steak and kidney had disappeared.

"Are you sober enough to answer a question?"

"Oh, yes."

"There was a piece on the news about Mr Bowman. They had the inquest today on the man who committed suicide. Mr Bowman had killed his daughter when he was drunk but got off with manslaughter. That's why the father decided to kill Mr Bowman the way he did. You always said it wasn't an accident. But then a policeman said the file had been closed on Margarite Pelouse. 'They weren't proposing to make any further inquiries'."

"Ah."

"You told them it was Mr Bowman who did that, didn't you?"

"More or less."

"All they had to do was tie up the loose ends?" Mr Pringle nodded. "What a lazy lot," said Mavis in disgust, "they obviously didn't bother. Makes you wonder why we pay all that income tax. It's jam roly-poly for afters, is that all right?" The two faces opposite smiled ecstatically.